"You see? You see how it is between us?"

His voice was ragged. He held her eyes deliberately as he massaged her breast through her shirt with infinite slowness.

Cathy shuddered and reached for his hand.

"Don't stop me," he breathed. "Don't stop yourself. Let me come with you. I want to know all about you . . . everything."

Cathy swallowed hard. They were like narcotics to each other. Even as she struggled to articulate her decision, her body yearned for him . . .

Dear Reader:

As the months go by, we continue to receive word from you that SECOND CHANCE AT LOVE romances are providing you with the kind of romantic entertainment you're looking for. In your letters you've voiced enthusiastic support for SECOND CHANCE AT LOVE, you've shared your thoughts on how personally meaningful the books are, and you've suggested ideas and changes for future books. Although we can't always reply to your letters as quickly as we'd like, please be assured that we appreciate your comments. Your thoughts are all-important to us!

We're glad many of you have come to associate SECOND CHANCE AT LOVE books with our butterfly trademark. We think the butterfly is a perfect symbol of the reaffirmation of life and thrilling new love that SECOND CHANCE AT LOVE heroines and heroes find together in each story. We hope you keep asking for the ''butterfly books,'' and that, when you buy one—whether by a favorite author or a talented new writer—you're sure of a good read. You can trust all SECOND CHANCE AT LOVE books to live up to the high standards of romantic fiction you've come to expect.

So happy reading, and keep your letters coming!

With warm wishes,

Ellen Edwards

Ellen Edwards
SECOND CHANCE AT LOVE
The Berkley/Jove Publishing Group
200 Madison Avenue
New York, NY 10016

SPRING FEVER
SIMONE HADARY

SECOND CHANCE AT LOVE
BOOK

Second Chance at Love books are published by
The Berkley/Jove Publishing Group
200 Madison Avenue, New York, NY 10016

SPRING FEVER

- 1 -

CATHY THOMAS DREW her face into an exaggerated frown and jammed her sneaker down hard on the accelerator. Another quick look in the rear-view mirror—just to make sure—then a gleeful smile replaced the frown as she watched the speedometer climb.

"For a woman who never breaks the rules," she said out loud, "you're doing a hell of a job!"

Sixty, sixty-five, seventy. The speedometer wavered at seventy-five, and Cathy's old blue Dart shuddered slightly, as if it were pleading with her to have mercy. Had she ever gone this fast before? No, never. Well, you could hardly go eighty with a car full of kids, right?

"Come on, girl, you can make eighty." Cathy glanced furtively into the rear-view mirror. The sun was just coming up, and she'd seen only three cars since checking out of the motel nearly an hour ago.

Speed. Speed was the answer. Cathy was laughing now. Certainly speed seemed to have a more healing effect than the tears she usually shed after seeing her ex-husband and their two sons, who lived with him and the new Mrs. Thomas. Well, she could scarcely call Sarah Thomas new, since she'd been married to Jed for nearly ten years, which was longer than Cathy had been married to him. Was it possible that she and Jed had been divorced for ten years?

Cathy nodded in answer to her own question. And, yes, it was possible that Bruce's voice was changing

1

at fourteen, that Brian at twelve was no longer a little boy, that her oldest daughter, Marilyn, was away at college, and that her youngest, Amy, at nine, was nearly as tall as she was. Yes, yes, yes. And in a few months she would be thirty-six years old. Yes, it was all true.

"Then why am I smiling?" Cathy mused as she rolled down the window and breathed in the fresh April air. The rolling Ohio fields were finally greening up, and here and there fields of brown earth had already been plowed.

She was smiling because for the first time in all the ten years of dropping off her daughters and visiting her sons she had not left her ex-husband's home feeling bitter and resentful. And that was saying a lot.

Actually, the custody arrangement had proved to be the right decision, though at the time the idea of her two sons moving out of her home to live with their father and his new wife had been unbearably painful. Ten years ago, when Jed had come to her and announced that he was leaving her for one of the nurses at his hospital, Cathy had had few alternatives. She had abandoned her own college education in her freshman year to marry Jed and then had fallen quite rapidly and regularly into the family way. She had been four months pregnant with Amy when Jed had announced he was filing for divorce.

"How did I live through it?" Her smile broadened, but she jammed her foot further down on the accelerator and the Dart shuddered again.

But she *had* lived through it, and except for the times when she was forced to see the domestic splendor in which Dr. Jed Thomas lived—the Tudor mansion, the rolling green lawn, the housekeeper, dogs, cats, ten-speed bikes, Mercedes, sailboat, and other sundry items of affluence—she quite relished and enjoyed her own simple life as an English instructor at Orange College. But how different it was for Bruce and Brian, living outside of Columbus in an exclusive neighborhood, than it was for Marilyn and Amy, who lived with her back on the beautiful but somewhat run-down farm outside of Orange.

Still, the arrangement had worked. The girls loved visiting Jed and Sarah, but they were always glad to return to the farm. The boys loved the farm too, but Cathy guessed they were equally eager to get back to the magnificent Tudor mansion. So much for divorce.

Cathy smiled to herself and checked the rear-view mirror once again. She did *not* need a speeding ticket . . . even if it would be her first. Imagine going all the way through life without a speeding ticket.

She grinned. She was dressed in snug jeans and a faded navy blue turtleneck, and with the wind whipping up her short, straight brown hair and not a speck of makeup on her pale, clear skin, she probably looked like a carefree coed off on a lark.

The old Dart was still shuddering, and Cathy let up on the gas. "Hey, girl, don't do me in today. Not when I'm feeling so . . ."

The Dart gasped and shook, and Cathy steered it off to the side of the road. The car came to a dead halt.

"I'll be damned." Cathy sat for a moment thinking, then climbed out. She lifted the hood and looked inside at the grease and mystery. Marilyn would have known what to do. For years Marilyn had been telling her, "Mom, you oughta know more about cars. Especially since you intend to drive the Dart till it dies."

"Well, Marilyn," Cathy saluted her absent daughter, who was spending spring vacation with a friend in Florida, "you were right."

Cathy stared again into the greasy abyss, then smiled suddenly and gazed out over the fertile fields. Her life was fine, just fine. Jed could have his fancy cars, caviar, and designer clothes. If she was honest with herself, she was more content with the quiet, rustic life. Yes, she was a born putterer, and the idea of converting the farm into a sedate, bucolic inn for people in search of solitude appealed enormously to her. Now that Marilyn was living away from home, it would really be possible to convert the house as well as the guest house.

Cathy reached inside the Dart for a Thermos of hot coffee. She perched herself on the front fender and sipped the coffee thoughtfully. If she was really clever and frugal, she could finish renovating and redecorating the guest house without depleting her entire savings. Then she could use the income from the two rentals to begin work on the main house. That meant that, barring the loss of her job at the college, by the time Amy graduated from high school, Cathy would have completely restored the farm and would be able to embark on an entirely new occupation as innkeeper.

And who knew? It might be possible to continue teaching several classes a week as well. Dr. Bradley, the head of the English Department, had told her only last week that for the fourth year in a row her Introduction to English Literature classes had been preferred by a majority of students. She would hate to give up teaching entirely. All of that positive feedback was very good for the ego!

Cathy drained the red plastic cup and screwed it back onto the Thermos. Whoever had written the song "Oh, What a Beautiful Morning" must have had just such a morning in mind. Except, of course, the corn wasn't "high as an elephant's eye" because it hadn't been planted yet. There was virtually no traffic on what was usually a very busy highway. Everyone else was still asleep on this brilliant Saturday morning. Well, someone would come along eventually.

Cathy sat crosslegged on the hood and considered the guest house. She had just started sanding the floors before taking Amy to visit her father. As soon as she completed that project, the first order of business would be adding a coat of polyurethane to preserve the beautiful pine floors. While that was drying she would go over wallpaper samples at Larrick's Hardware. She was leaning toward a French provincial flower pattern—little blue cornflowers on a white background with touches of violet, very crisp and springy. Oh, these next two weeks were going to be fun!

"Hey!" Cathy leaped off the fender as a dark green sports car whizzed by. "Damn!" she muttered halfheartedly. Actually she was enjoying her roadside visit.

She climbed back onto the fender and poured herself another cup of coffee. A moment later the small green car backed into view, and a young man leaned out the window.

"You're not supposed to back up on the highway," Cathy shouted, jumping down. "You'll get a ticket."

"You'll get a ticket for speeding." The young man

leaned out the car window and grinned at her as he pulled his car alongside of the Dart. "You were going eighty back there. You passed me."

"I didn't pass you." Cathy sloshed the hot coffee onto her jeans and winced.

The young man got out of his car. He was laughing at her. "You could get fired."

"What do you mean?" Cathy smiled back into his teasing blue eyes, but he only hooked his thumbs in his belt loops and leaned his lanky, young body against the green sports car. He was still chuckling.

"Why were you going so fast?" His blue eyes moved slowly down her body and returned to study her face with the same self-assured amusement.

At the most he was in his mid-twenties, Cathy surmised, which was older than most of the students at Orange College. There was something familiar about him, or maybe... yes, it was his green roadster that looked familiar. She had seen the car parked on campus.

She met his amused gaze and was shocked at her shortness of breath as their eyes locked for an instant.

"I don't know what's wrong." She gestured vaguely at the old Dart. A warm, fluttering numbness seemed to be seeping into her body, but she managed to walk calmly to the hood and lift it easily.

"Why were you speeding?" The man moved next to her and peered into the engine.

Cathy could feel the heat from his body. "I was celebrating," she replied without thinking.

The man laughed as if he understood perfectly, and Cathy felt her skin prickle with enjoyment. She grinned up at him. "You know what I mean?"

"On a deserted highway with no one to endanger and only you at the controls...the power of the engine, the exhilaration of being utterly in control." He nodded his curly blond head. "I understand."

"I never did it before," Cathy admitted.

"I didn't think you were the type." He studied her intently. "Maybe it's unimaginative of me, but an English Literature professor who speeds? What would Wordsworth say?"

"I don't know you," Cathy began.

"You do now." He reached for her hand and shook it. "Robbie Darrow."

"Cathy Thomas."

Robbie continued holding her hand as he explained that he had enrolled at Orange in January and that, at twenty-five, he was the oldest student extant. He was finishing up the last semester of his bachelor's degree.

"I've noticed you," he said, finally dropping her hand. "You win the prettiest professor award hands down."

Cathy blushed. Twenty-five was too young.

"Thank you." She nodded perfunctorily and tried to adopt a more distant manner, one more commensurate with her thirty-five years and her position on the Orange faculty.

"I'll have a look at this." Robbie began tapping and jabbing at the maze of wires under the hood. Cathy took a deep breath and moved several feet away from him, hoping distance would dispel the almost joyous anticipation she felt in his presence. This was absurd, ridiculous. Scenes from a movie that had been popular in her youth flashed through her mind—older woman seduces young man. Good Lord! It was spring, and she was losing her mind!

The sensations that raged through her body were embarrassing her, and one look at Robbie Darrow told her that he was the sort of young man who was not unfamiliar with such positive responses from women. He was tall, maybe a little over six feet, and he had the grace of an athlete, a tennis player or swimmer, she guessed. No, she amended, he had the grace of the rich, of a young man who spent his summers sailing and sunning. She could visualize his lean, muscular legs in white tennis shorts.

Cathy closed her eyes against the thought. Good grief, it wasn't as if she didn't see young men all the time. Her classes were filled with them. Boys, she called them. And yes, she knew that one of the reasons so many male students signed up for her class was because they liked having a young*ish*, pretty*ish* teacher. So it wasn't a question of never being around young men.

She looked back at Robbie Darrow, whose blond head was now obscured as he bent over the engine. He was wearing jeans and a light blue cashmere sweater, tennis shoes and white socks. There was nothing out of the ordinary in his dress, only the way he wore the clothes, with casual elegance. Such country-club elegance would be more suitable on the campus at Princeton than in Orange.

So why was he here? Orange was a good school but not one that attracted rich easterners who drove green sports cars.

Cathy was totally absorbed in her curiosity about

Robbie Darrow as he moved from the hood and slid into the front seat of the Dart. She pulled herself to her feet and stood with her hands on her hips. Robbie tried unsuccessfully to start the car. To her chagrin, she realized she was pleased. Imagine, after years of pampering and coddling the old car, she was heartlessly throwing it over for...

She gave herself a mental shake as Robbie approached her. "No luck. Looks like the alternator's gone. I'll give you a lift into Orange."

"Right." Cathy swallowed and ran back to her car to gather up her purse and canvas overnight bag. Robbie was holding the door of his car open for her, and as she slipped into the passenger's seat, she felt his warm eyes on her.

"I know a great place for champagne and waffles." He turned to her as he slipped the key into the ignition.

"I should get home." Cathy's heart was racing. Now panic was edging out her previous giddiness. "I have to phone about the car. I've got tons of painting. I'm redoing a building on my place."

"Aren't you hungry?" Robbie leaned over and brought his face very close to hers. His breath was sweet and warm. He smelled faintly of soap.

Cathy listened to the low idling of the car. It seemed an eternity before she could speak. "Yes, but..."

She glanced up into his clear blue eyes, and for several moments it seemed that the silence of the early spring morning was swirling around them, encompassing them in a separate world. He was looking at her with such serious intensity that she couldn't tear her eyes away.

"I have so much work to do," she added lamely.

"But you need energy, sustenance." He scanned her face. "I guarantee you won't regret it. You'll get more for your mileage if you fill up in the A.M. What's that saying?"

"I don't know." Cathy felt a smile begin to play around her mouth as he wrinkled his nose in an effort to recall some scrap of information that would convince her. She was flattered by his determination, but more than that she was intrigued.

"I know!" Robbie snapped his fingers enthusiastically. "A person should eat like an emperor in the morning, a king at noon, and—"

"A beggar at night," Cathy supplied, smiling.

"Right!" Robbie pumped her hand enthusiastically, as if they had made an important discovery. Her hand felt small in his large, warm one. His long, tapered fingers pressed her knuckles together. The connection between them was electrifying. The soft kneading of his fingers made her catch her breath. She didn't want to feel these things. She snatched her hand away. He was staring at her with the unabashed hunger of a young animal.

"I wish you'd have breakfast with me." The simple statement elicited a new, more insistent yearning in her. Cathy wavered. Something in his expression was making it almost impossible to turn him down.

She felt a rush of warm pleasure again as he reached for her hand. "I'd like to kiss you," he said with the same disarming simplicity.

Cathy was caught completely off guard. She blinked at him, bewildered. Finally she laughed and shook her head. "How can you toss off such non sequiturs at this hour?"

Robbie took her rejection with a good-natured grin. "Do you have rules or something? No kissing before nine o'clock?"

Cathy laughed again, relieved that the conversation had turned light and teasing.

"What about after nine?" he asked. "It'll take us about twenty minutes to get to the inn."

"You're joking." Cathy tossed her head as he shifted the car into gear, and they shot out onto the highway.

"No." Robbie glanced sideways at her.

"How do you know I'm not married?" Cathy challenged with a smile.

"You're not wearing a wedding ring."

"Maybe I took it off," she chirped, enjoying the exchange.

"No you didn't." Robbie reached over and patted her thigh. It was a friendly pat, nothing offensive, like the affectionate paw of a young puppy. Lord, he was young!

"Well, I'm not married." Cathy said decisively, deciding to put an end to their flirtatious repartee. "I'm divorced and . . . and I have a family and I think all that speed went to my head. And I . . . I don't get involved with students. It's against the rules."

"I'm atypical," Robbie chortled. "If you don't get involved with students, I'll quit school. I'm flexible."

"You're crazy." Cathy tried not to smile. There was a carefree lustiness in his manner that was positively bewitching.

"You're crazy too." Robbie smiled at her.

"I really can't take time for breakfast," Cathy said after a moment.

"Yes you can." She sent him an exasperated look,

which he ignored, then settled back in her seat. Since
he wasn't going to take no for an answer, she might
as well enjoy herself.

- 2 -

BY THE TIME the green MG wound its way up the steep driveway to the Hilltop Inn, Cathy had regained her composure. She excused herself to phone the tow service in Orange and stopped briefly in the ladies' room. Looking in the mirror, she saw that her brown hair was tousled from the ride in Robbie's convertible, but that her face was flushed and more relaxed than she had seen it in years. *Stop,* she cautioned herself. *You're just flattered because a handsome young man thinks you're kind of cute. Don't let it go to your head. Don't get carried away.*

She rejoined Robbie in the small glassed-in dining room that overlooked a rushing stream. He was smiling and gazing out at the woods, which were just beginning to turn a delicate spring green. She noted champagne in a silver ice bucket and two glasses brimming with the pale, bubbly liquid. A little chickadee swooped near the window, and Robbie gave a low chuckle and mumbled something to the bird.

"Talking to birds?" Cathy took her seat, feeling unaccountably pleased to be in his company.

He turned to her and raised his glass without a word. Cathy nervously followed suit, touching the fluted champagne glass to his and trying desperately to think of a casual toast that would relegate their friendship to safer territory.

"To love," Robbie toasted.

"To common sense." Cathy gave him a critical look as she took a sip of champagne. "Listen," she began, putting down her glass and leaning intently across the small table, "you really have the wrong idea. I really don't date . . . or whatever you want to call it . . . students. You're much younger than I am."

"What are you afraid of?" Robbie's blue eyes were serious.

"I'm not afraid!" Cathy bristled, then smiled quickly to dispel the impression that he had confused her. "I'm not afraid," she repeated. "I just think you—"

"You want to make love to me."

Cathy gulped. She felt bewildered and helpless in the face of his candor.

"You do," he insisted. He sipped his champagne casually. His confidence was beginning to make her feel uneasy.

"You have no idea how old I am." She gave him a pointed look.

"It doesn't matter." Robbie met her eyes steadily. "I'd say you're about twenty-eight. Three years difference—big deal!"

Cathy smiled smugly.

"You're older? Okay. It still doesn't matter. You can't be hung up on that convention. You mean to tell me if I were some gray-haired old man you'd go to bed with—"

"We're not really discussing that," Cathy interrupted sharply. He nodded and looked out the window.

What were they discussing anyway? she wondered. She had no intention of getting involved with him for a lot of reasons, only one of which was because he was a student and she was a professor. Dating students was more than frowned upon at Orange College. There was an unwritten rule against it.

"You look worried." She glanced up to find Robbie studying her closely.

"No." Cathy shrugged and shook her head.

"Your face is an open book," he teased gently.

"Look who's talking." Cathy laughed into his ingenuous young face. Beneath the table she could feel his knees grazing hers. She shifted uncomfortably and reached for her champagne glass, hoping he didn't notice the blush of color on her face.

"You're as young as you want to be," Robbie observed wryly.

Cathy gave him a fleeting glance. There was a certain maturity about him, which was confusing because he looked so damned young. It occurred to her that her overwhelming interest in him was probably a result of a lack of interesting male companionship in her life lately. For years she had been so serious, so responsible, so intent on building a good, solid life for herself and her children. It suddenly occurred to her that she'd never taken the time to really enjoy life.

"Do you like the circus?" Robbie asked softly, catching her off balance once again.

"What?"

"Circuses. Do you like them?"

"I guess so." She eyed him warily.

"I think we should go. Today. I think you need to see clowns tumbling and elephants jumping through hoops. For that matter, I think I need to, too." Robbie caught her eye and held it.

"I'm thirty-three . . ." Cathy winced at the lie. Why had she bothered to knock two measly years off her age?

"That's too old for me," said Robbie with mock horror, pretending to stand up to leave. "I'll get you home as soon as we eat our waffles. Maybe you should ride in the back seat."

Cathy laughed. He really was irresistible. She studied him surreptitiously as the waitress placed steaming plates of waffles and sausage in front of them. Even for twenty-five he had an uncommonly young, almost guileless face. Yet his manner suggested a complexity and maturity that she didn't often find in her male students. There was a wily sophistication in Robbie's manner that implied experience and knowledge, probably not of an academic nature. Yes, something set him apart from other students, from other people for that matter. Maybe it was his candor, the way he went straight to the heart of the matter—even when the subject was sex.

He was of a different generation. Cathy knew that sexual liaisons were formed under the most extraordinary circumstances among her students. For many of them there simply were no rules. She wondered what Robbie Darrow's rules were.

"Yum!" Robbie poured more maple syrup on his waffles.

"They're going to float away," Cathy teased.

"The only reason to eat waffles is for the syrup." He refilled their champagne glasses.

"I have so much work to do today," Cathy protested. "I won't be able to walk after eating all of this."

"Perhaps you should try something other than walking, working, and other forms of drudgery for a change."

He savored a bite of waffle, but his expression suggested that he was thinking of a far more satisfying adventure than eating breakfast. His blue eyes rested often on Cathy as he devoured the plate of waffles and waved to the waitress to bring him another order.

"And a glass of milk," he called.

"With champagne?" Cathy gasped.

Robbie grinned. "You'll find I often don't follow the rules."

"Oh." Cathy shook her head. "I'll find that out, will I?"

"I think so." Robbie gave her a meaningful glance that made her stomach leap.

Cathy directed her attention back to her food, but her pulse quickened as she indulged in a fleeting image. What would it be like to make love with this man? She was seized by the idea. She clutched her fork and jabbed at the waffle. She knew Robbie was staring at her, openly studying her, evaluating her and, yes, probably imagining the same thing she was— the two of them alone, together.

"So . . ." Cathy washed down the waffle with a gulp of champagne. "What brought you onto the highway so early in the morning?"

"I drove all night." Robbie smiled.

"All night?" Cathy was skeptical. He certainly didn't appear frazzled or exhausted, not even slightly rumpled.

"Yes." He nodded. "My folks live in Wilbur, Connecticut, home of executive commuters to New York."

"I've heard of it, of course." Cathy had detected a certain bitterness in his voice. Suddenly his face took on a somber expression, and for the first time she fully perceived the maturity she had only vaguely detected before. She was more curious than she had been about a man in...maybe ever. Now that was silly. She told herself not to exaggerate.

"You don't like Wilbur?"

"How did you guess?" Robbie flashed one of his most charming smiles at the waitress as she set another plate of waffles in front of him. He looked up at Cathy after flooding the plate with maple syrup. "Let's say I make my visits as brief as possible."

Cathy waited until he was nearly finished eating before asking the next question.

"You went home to visit your family over spring vacation and you're back already?"

"You got it!" Robbie wiped his mouth with his napkin. "Do I dare order another?"

"You're a growing boy..."

"Not a boy." He pinned her with his gaze. "For an intelligent woman you're certainly...how can I say it nicely?"

"I'm sorry," Cathy apologized. "That was a dumb remark. Not sexist or racist but...agist. I have an uncle who's seventy-one, and he eats much more than you do."

"Apology accepted." Robbie regarded her seriously. "You're sensitive about your age?"

"No!" Cathy winced at her overzealous protest, but it was true. She had never been sensitive about her age before. Only now, after meeting twenty-five-year-old Robbie Darrow, did thirty-five suddenly seem ancient.

"How does that ad go? 'You're not getting older, you're getting better'?" Robbie chuckled softly. "I'm sure it's true. They say women reach their full sexual capacity in their thirties. Men reach it earlier. It seems to me that the perfect combination is—"

"Do you mind if we change the subject?" Cathy interrupted with a wry smile. She was beginning to feel tipsy from the champagne, and that combined with his sex-oriented conversation was making her almost dizzy with desire.

"What shall we talk about?" Robbie leaned across the table and peered up at her. "I'll talk about anything you like. Politics? I'm good at talking politics. Business? I've read the *Wall Street Journal* since I was eleven. I know a bit about art. I've only been to the ballet four times, but I go to concerts regularly. I don't like football or basketball, but I'm an avid Yankee fan. We'll discuss whatever you—"

"How come you're full of so much energy if you drove all night?" Cathy interrupted him.

"Just glad to get away from . . . oh, I don't know." He shook his head. "I just feel better out here than back there, more like myself. There's so much money in Wilbur that everyone's pretty much alike. It's a homogeneous community. Everybody's raised to be an overachiever. The pressure's tremendous. You feel it walking down the street. I'm convinced you can't grow up with all of that eastern affluence and not be damaged."

"What do you mean?" Cathy studied him intently.

Robbie Darrow was in no way a typical Orange College student. There was an almost mysterious dichotomy between his youthful country-club good looks and the biting, slightly cynical tone that occasionally crept into his voice.

"I mean," he continued thoughtfully, "that I'm a product of such an environment. My father gave me everything. Or *almost* everything. Does that sound ungrateful? Of course I am grateful for much of what he gave me. What I'm saying is I'm a typical eastern rich kid. You know, private schools, summers at Camp Watobottomy in Maine or on the French Riviera. Charge accounts, cars, boats. An overabundance of material goods lavished on the progeny." Robbie stared coolly out the window, his jaw set in a tense, unyielding line.

This, Cathy thought, was not a typical youthful tirade against one's parents. Naturally in her position she had heard many such complaints. So far her own children hadn't rebelled, but she believed it was inevitable that they would eventually break away and differ from many of the values she held.

Robbie seemed to be reacting in a different way, against something more far-reaching and complex. He was no disgruntled, griping kid. She sensed in his attitude both deep hurt and deep commitment. She smiled briefly.

"In other words"—she tapped him lightly on the arm—"you don't spend much time at home because it's . . . rather empty."

"It always shocks me." Robbie turned back to her. "I'm twenty-five. I should be able to accept the way things are by now. But I always expect that this time it will be different. You know, the happy family sitting around the dinner table laughing and joking. Instead, I haven't even seen my younger sister in two years. They sent her to boarding school when she was eight. My two older brothers were already grown up when I was very young. They've pretty much deserted the familial ship. Oh, they're both chips off the old block—like my father, I mean. Both of them are workaholics, both divorced and remarried. I'm the black sheep."

"You don't look like a black sheep." Cathy smiled warmly.

"I don't usually run off at the mouth like this," Robbie said apologetically.

"Maybe you're tired."

"No." Robbie shook his head. "It's not the fatigue, it's the company. You're easy to talk to."

"You're easy to listen to," Cathy said without thinking, then looked away. For a moment they had been just two people talking. She wanted to know more about him, but her acute physical awareness of him made her uncomfortable. At the same time she felt more alive than she had in months.

"My dad's rich," Robbie went on. "That's the only way to describe him. He has a very wealthy lifestyle. My brothers reacted to the family wealth by competing against my father, showing him up, making more money, buying up more companies, marrying more beautiful women. Neither one needs or wants any part of Darrow Enterprises, the conglomerate label for my father's various investments. So guess who that leaves to carry on the family business?"

Cathy pointed at Robbie, and he laughed and nodded. "Right. The black sheep. The dropout. The kid who quit Harvard twice."

"You're making me dizzy." Cathy shook her head. "Maybe it's the champagne."

"No, it's probably me and my story. It makes me dizzy too. I can't believe I'm telling you all this."

"Why did you quit Harvard?" Cathy asked.

"I got close to graduating, then went off on some tangent. Something else would pique my interest— or so I thought at the time. The last time I almost graduated was four years ago, when I was twenty-one. Now I see that it was really a lack of discipline, and a reluctance to be responsible for myself. I was a spoiled rich kid. Right down the line I was your Wilbur, Connecticut stereotype."

"And something changed you?" Cathy inquired, fascinated.

"I want more than my father, more than my brothers. That's why I drive when I go back home. I want the reality of the miles, the distance between places. I want to see the way spring is touching the farmlands in Pennsylvania. I want to see the land change, and I even want my muscles to ache. Oh, sometimes I can't spare the time to drive instead of fly. But I basically believe that all this speed, this obsession to accomplish, is just a meaningless way to devour time. I want to live my life, not devour it. At the same time I have certain goals. My father owns a number of factories in this part of Ohio. Unless I alienate him beyond repair, it looks like I'll be heir to the Darrow empire. I don't want to run it from Connecticut and New York."

"So you came to Orange College to—"

"To get to know the factories and the people who work in them. To learn something about the way things *really* are. I'm no sucker idealist. I have an ulterior motive, though I like to think my motives are more humane than my father's."

Cathy nodded. "And what does your father think of all this?"

Robbie smiled. "He's appalled because I've decided to graduate from a college nobody has ever heard of. As far as he's concerned, it's like drinking cheap whiskey when you could have Chivas Regal."

Cathy laughed at the analogy. "But it makes sense to you?"

"Damn right!" Robbie exclaimed. "I'm fed up with labels. If you graduate from Harvard, everybody puts a label on you, doors open to you, and people assume they know where you come from and what you're capable of. Same with clothes—labels on every damn thing. People seem to think labels will make them feel secure. I've gone out with women who wouldn't buy a pair of jeans unless they had the right label on them.

"It's the person I'm interested in, not the label," he continued. "I noticed right off when you bent over your poor car that you don't have the right label on your jeans. However, you do have—" His voice had become low and husky, though his eyes danced.

"You're terrible!" Cathy interrupted, laughing.

Robbie laughed with her. "Now I have another point to make."

"Be my guest." Cathy drained the rest of her champagne. It amazed her how their conversation had gone from very serious to very silly, yet all with an underlying feeling of intimacy. She felt she understood a great deal about Robbie Darrow. Oddly enough, she had the feeling he understood something about her too. She enjoyed his light teasing. Even his very forthright flirting wasn't offensive.

"The point is"—Robbie eyed her narrowly—"that according to your rules—"

"My rules?" Cathy interrupted.

"According to your rules," Robbie went on, "my father, Raymond the Terrible, would be a more appropriate match for you."

"We're not talking about matches." Cathy frowned.

"But we both know women need looking after, and obviously an older man has greater—"

"What do you mean looking after?" Cathy interrupted again.

"Just what I said," Robbie continued with a stern expression. "Women need guidance, experience, and . . ."

He paused and looked expectantly at Cathy. She cocked her head to one side, not sure if he was teasing.

"I don't need guidance," she said seriously.

Robbie burst out laughing. "Of course you don't! And you certainly don't need my father. He's fifty years old, quite distinguished, and in excellent shape from playing tennis. His new wife is your age."

"What's your point?" Cathy felt herself tensing up. She knew perfectly well what his point was, though he had a rather circuitous manner of stating it. Her objection to him because of the difference in their ages was ridiculous. And his implied point that she had far more in common with him than she did with his father was well taken. But where did that leave her?

If she was honest, she would look him straight in the eye and say she would like nothing better than to sit there all day talking with him. But that was only a means to something else, some other desire that had taken hold the moment she'd laid eyes on him. Had it been only the beauty of the spring morning, the exhilaration of speeding down an empty highway, that had opened her in this strange way? Or was there really something special in the way they were communicating?

She couldn't trust her feelings. Twenty-five years old. Her own daughter was a more appropriate age. Cathy caught herself. She hadn't even told him about Marilyn. What would he think if he knew she had a seventeen-year-old daughter?

Without answering her previous question, he reached for his wallet. She protested. After all, he had done her a favor by driving her back to Orange. If it hadn't been for him she might have been stranded on the highway for hours.

"No." Robbie shook his head firmly and guided her out of the inn. "And not because you're a woman."

"I should hope not." Cathy felt a warm flush cover her cheeks as he put his arm around her and they walked across the gravel parking lot to his car.

"The reason is because I invited you." He opened the door for her. "You were going to go home and have a dry piece of toast and tea with milk."

"What?" Cathy cried. Is that how he saw her, as a tight, pinched person who would eat dry toast and tea?

He stood away from her, laughing at her perplexed expression. Then, just as she was about to slip into the front seat, he whisked her into his arms and pressed her against his lean body. "I don't think you're the dry toast type at all," he murmured. "On the contrary..."

Cathy gave in to the demands of his strong arms, which wrapped tightly around her until she felt herself molded against him. Her heart raced wildly as she recognized and surrendered to her need for him. She tried telling herself the champagne was responsible for her foolish behavior, but her mind was as clear as ever. Still, nothing seemed to matter except the feel of his body, which seemed to enfold and protect her.

There were countless reasons why this was wrong, not the least of which was that they were standing in broad daylight in a public place. Yet nothing could force her to tear herself away from him. They stood clutching each other, pressing so deeply against each other that it seemed to Cathy she could feel the blood coursing through his body. His heart thundered under her ear, which was pressed firmly against his chest. His hard thighs pressed against her legs, and she felt a throbbing intensity as he became aroused in her embrace.

They swayed together, as if magnetized and unable to pull apart. Cathy's body was tingling, and a warm dizziness was about to overtake her when Robbie finally pulled away. They stared at each other, speechless. She couldn't hide from him. She was sure he could read every emotion in her face.

In silence he helped her into the car, then stared

straight ahead as he drove. Neither of them spoke until they entered the Orange city limits.

"Make a right at the first traffic light." Cathy's voice was faint. The fifteen-minute drive had barely dulled the agonizing desire that still raged through her body. Although Robbie sat across the seat from her, she could almost feel the heat emanating from him. She clenched her fists and fought back her feelings.

She had heard of women her age getting involved with younger men. She knew the risks involved. But the longing would not die. Never in her life had she wanted a man the way she wanted Robbie Darrow.

When he shifted the car into first gear to pull into the dirt lane that led to her house, she put her hand on his arm and stopped him.

"I'll get out here." She couldn't risk looking into his eyes, knowing what she would see there. "I . . . I have to pick up the mail."

She started to open the door, but he stopped her. Hadn't she known he would?

"When can I see you?" His voice was thick with passion. She knew he felt as tortured as she did. What if she led him up the stairs to her room? What if they pulled the blinds down and she spread herself before him on the brass bed? She was mad!

She pulled away from him. "You've been very kind. I . . ." Cathy blinked in bewilderment as Robbie jumped out of the car, ran around, and flung open her door. He pulled her out of the front seat and seared his body against hers.

Once, she thought, just once and then it would be over. One kiss. There could be no harm in one kiss.

Robbie's mouth sought hers forcefully. If she'd had any doubts before, they were banished now. This was no youthful lover. His full lips surrounded her, his tongue like a fiery brand inside her mouth, tasting her, savoring her. She gasped joyously as a portion of her intense desire was fulfilled by the slow stroking of his tongue. She turned into his embrace, reveling in the way her breasts tingled against his steely chest.

His hands swept down the sides of her body, then moved slowly over her full hips, her tiny waist, and upward to her breasts.

"You see? You see how it is between us?" His voice was ragged, a growl of desire. He held her eyes deliberately as he massaged her breast through her shirt with infinite slowness.

Cathy shuddered and reached for his hand.

"Don't stop me," he breathed. "Don't stop yourself. Let me come with you. I want to know all about you . . . everything."

Cathy swallowed hard. They were like narcotics to each other. Even as she struggled to articulate her decision, her body yearned for him. Her hands began to slowly and rhythmically rub the small of his back. The muscles there were fine and hard. She closed her eyes and moved her hands around his waist, feeling his tight abdomen. Suddenly she jerked her hands away as if she had been burned.

"I probably am a fool," she said tightly, backing away from him. What could she say? Her body was still throbbing with awareness.

"Whatever you think." He looked down at his shoes. His arms hung limply at his sides.

"I think you should go," Cathy whispered.

"All right." Robbie nodded and walked back around to the driver's seat. Cathy didn't wait. She ran up the dirt lane, biting her lip to keep from crying.

- 3 -

CATHY STOOD UNDER a scalding shower and allowed the water to beat down on her body, hoping that so much heat from the outside would subdue the torrid pulsing inside. Spring fever, that's what it was. She turned her back against the spray and felt hot needles on her back. What she wanted to feel was Robbie's hands. She closed her eyes against the thought.

She turned off the water and stepped out of the old tub onto the black and white tiled floor. She wiped the steam off the bathroom mirror and studied her flushed face. Her green eyes were bright with excitement, and her quizzical expression was tinged with an eagerness she hadn't felt in a long time.

She backed away from the mirror and stared at her body. Her breasts were small, but nicely shaped and firm. Her pink nipples were ripe and hard with the same anticipation and expectancy she read in her face. Her waist, she was proud to say, was precisely the same measurement it had been when she was eighteen years old, and if an added layer had formed around her hips, at least the flesh remained taut and smooth. Her breathing accelerated. She had never been so acutely aware of her body.

With an impatient grimace she flounced into her bedroom, which was in its usual state of disarray. With teaching, mothering, gardening, and renovating the old house to occupy her time, she'd put aside the finer aspects of domesticity. When Marilyn was still home she had been in charge of vacuuming and general cleaning, but since she was off at college Cathy was lucky if she found one day a month in which to accomplish those tasks.

She looked around the room in disgust, trying to see it through Robbie Darrow's eyes. Robbie, who had lived in a Wilbur mansion and probably been chauffeured around New York City in his father's limousine. The disparity between their lives was as great as the disparity in their ages.

Stop thinking about him, Cathy told herself as she pulled on a clean pair of jeans.

"Damn, damn, damn," she cursed under her breath as she pulled on a paint-stained Orange College sweatshirt. She hurried out of her bedroom, past Amy's room, and down the steep flight of stairs to the living room. After phoning the garage to check on the progress of her poor Dart—it had just arrived on the tow truck—she threw herself into her first project of the day—sanding the floor in the guest house.

As she passed through the kitchen, she resisted the temptation to make herself a cup of tea and sit at the table daydreaming. Tea had taken on new, negative connotations. She wondered if she would ever be able to drink it without thinking of Robbie, without thinking of herself as tottering on the brink of senility. Oh, what a silly thought!

She slammed the kitchen door shut and stood on the back porch sniffing the warm April air. It was almost noon and the temperature, she noted on the outdoor thermometer, was hovering around seventy. Unseasonably warm. Maybe that was why she felt so lethargic, so languid, so... *get a grip on yourself, Cathy*. A crush, that's all it was. Just a crush.

Cathy plugged in the industrial sander she had rented and steadied herself before switching it on. The machine was hard to use, especially for someone of her petite build. The man at the rental agency had warned her that she wouldn't be able to control it, but so far she had managed. She gripped the handle with both hands and concentrated on removing the layers of old varnish without gouging the wood.

A few hours later Cathy finished vacuuming the residue from the sanding. She glanced at her watch, pleased that so much time had passed without a single thought of Robbie Darrow. Why, she felt practically normal.

She frowned. What did that mean, practically normal? She lugged the machine onto the tiny porch that had been added to the guest house. Suddenly she felt quite drained, almost depressed.

She went into the kitchen, put on the tea kettle, and began preparing lunch. Without her car she was really hampered. She wouldn't be able to return the rented machine or go to Larrick's to pick up the wallpaper. And tomorrow was Sunday, which meant that her redecorating schedule was already off. If only she hadn't allowed herself to be coerced into going for a champagne breakfast with Robbie. If only...

The ring of the telephone startled her so much that she actually jumped and dropped her teabag on the floor. Instantly her heart began to pound, which irritated her further. She answered the phone with a clipped "Hello."

"Hi." Robbie's voice sent a shiver of excitement

up her spine. "How's the sanding coming along?"

"I just finished." Cathy twisted the phone cord in one hand and shifted from foot to foot.

"Anything I can do to help?"

"Can't think of a thing," she replied pertly.

"Cathy..." His voice was lower now, and she sensed he was having difficulty getting the words out, but she didn't help him. After a moment he continued. "Cathy, why don't we go for a bite somewhere after you've finished working. Pizza...anything. You won't want to cook after slaving away all day."

"That's nice of you"—Cathy cut off a phony smile; after all, he couldn't see her—"but I really can't. Robbie, I really do appreciate your...coming to my rescue so to speak, but I really don't think it would be appropriate for you, a student, and I, a professor, to see each other. I'm quite sure I don't want to...to get involved."

"We're already involved," Robbie replied matter-of-factly.

Cathy ran her hand through her hair. "No we're not," she answered. "I'm sorry...I have to go."

She hung up, walked briskly over to the whistling tea kettle and, with an air of defiance, poured herself a cup of tea.

By four o'clock that afternoon she felt she had regained her equilibrium. She had given the guest-room floors a coat of polyurethane and, suddenly seized by a burst of energy, had vacuumed the entire house. Still, an empty evening loomed ahead of her, not to mention the next day.

She was sitting in an old rocker on the back porch

trying to think up some new chore to distract herself with, when Susan Wilcox's station wagon bumped up the driveway and choked to a stop.

"Hi!" Cathy leaped off the porch and ran to greet her friend. "Where's the gang?" She peered inside the car, which was usually brimming with Susan's four young children and their golden retriever.

Susan lumbered out of the car, exaggerating the exhaustion which she no doubt really felt. "Do you have anything sweet to eat?" the plump, dark-haired woman asked. "I'm in my afternoon slump. I need a fix of sugar. If you don't have a cookie, I'll just have a tablespoon straight from the bowl."

Cathy giggled and put her arm around Susan as they walked to the porch. Susan shook her head as she collapsed on the porch swing, which was in sore need of repainting.

"Ted took all four little demons over to Columbus to the circus. I declined." Susan smiled. "Spring fever's got me or low blood sugar or something. I feel old. You know, Cathy, you were real smart to have kids as young as you did."

Cathy shrugged. She had heard this theory of Susan's before.

"We're the same age," Susan espoused, "but my oldest is Amy's age. I've got years of mothering ahead of me. I don't think I'm going to make it."

Cathy laughed. "How 'bout some tea? I can offer you that or there might be some of Amy's cookies left."

"I'm on a diet." Susan pulled her hefty body to attention. "A fruity diet. Only fruit. It sounded great, you know, all that sweet fructose. Only it's not great."

"Spring fever," Cathy diagnosed. "I've had a case of it myself today." Her body trembled slightly as her words triggered a memory of Robbie's solid body pressing into hers. For an instant she felt overcome with dizziness. She glanced quickly at Susan, but the other woman was rummaging around in her large handbag.

"Where's Mike?" Susan asked without looking up.

"I'm not seeing much of him anymore," Cathy answered.

Susan looked up abruptly. "But the two of you are coming over for dinner this week, aren't you?"

"Oh, yes." Cathy looked off in the distance to a slope of daffodils that were just coming into bloom. "It's just that we're trying not to make it a regular thing."

"Your idea, not Mike's," Susan replied critically. "Cathy, you're nuts if you . . . well, I know it's none of my business, but the guy's crazy about you. You have so much in common."

"For now I'm just not interested in getting into a habitual. . . ." Cathy's voice faded. Basketball coach Mike O'Sullivan was Orange College's most sought-after man. He was thirty-eight, recently divorced, red-haired, and handsome enough to have many coeds conniving to be in his presence.

"Oh, you!" Susan scolded. "You're never interested in anything habitual. Well, you never can tell. I knew Ted for three years before I finally got the message. Honest. I saw him every day for three years and suddenly one day out of the blue my heart started skipping beats. It was really weird. To each his own, that's what I say. Just don't burn your bridges, kiddo."

"Oh, I won't," Cathy assured her, suddenly tense. Wasn't that precisely what she had done with Robbie Darrow, burned her bridges? Sudden panic swept over her. What if he never called again?

". . . So that's why I'm here," Susan's voice interrupted Cathy's thoughts, and she turned to her friend with an apologetic smile. "You okay?" Susan inquired. "Did you have a rough time leaving Amy with Jed or something?"

"No, it was fine," Cathy said. "I guess I'm tired. I drove back early this morning, my car broke down—it's been a hectic day."

"So!" Susan clapped her hands together and leaned conspiratorially forward on the porch swing. "Here's my news. Someone called me at the real estate office today and made an offer on the farm."

"What farm?" Cathy asked, suddenly alert.

"*Your* farm."

"But I don't want to sell. I love this place. Susan, you know how much I love this crumbling old—"

"That's the point, sweetie. It's crumbling. I know you have these big plans for restoring it, but how on earth are you going to afford it on your salary? Bit by bit, I know. First the guest house, then this, then that. You'll be a hundred and nine before you open your doors for business."

"Thanks a lot," Cathy said petulantly.

"Hey, I'm sorry." Susan patted Cathy's knee. "You know I'm your biggest fan. Nobody has the energy and pizzazz that you have. But wait till you hear the offer, Cath. It's incredible. You could buy a place that doesn't need this much work. You could open your inn next year!"

Cathy shook her head. "I'm not interested. Not at any price."

"Five hundred thousand dollars." Susan was jubilant.

Cathy stared at her, incredulous.

"I told you." Susan grinned. "Some offer, huh?"

Cathy looked back to the daffodils, which were wafting gently in the late afternoon sun. The sum of money meant absolutely nothing to her. For the second time that day she decided to do something she might regret later.

"No dice," she told Susan, whose mouth flew open in surprise. Then the telephone rang, and Cathy ran inside to answer it. She heard the door slam as Susan followed her inside and turned to see her staring at her with the same comical expression of disbelief on her chubby face.

"Hello?" Cathy answered with her usual gusto, but her manner changed when Robbie identified himself and proposed dinner at his apartment.

"Look, I told you," Cathy said in a hushed voice, "I can't. I don't want to see you. There's no point. Really, I'm not just saying this, I mean it!"

She replaced the receiver and turned to meet Susan's curious gaze. No one loved sniffing out new romances more than Susan Wilcox.

"So?" Susan eyed Cathy with a knowing smile.

"I met a . . . a man." Cathy shrugged. "It's nothing. He . . . he's just being persistent."

"Hey, kiddo." Susan squinted at Cathy. "I don't

believe you. I heard your voice. I never heard you talk to Mike O'Sullivan that way."

"What way?" Cathy demanded, bristling. "I turned him down. I was abrupt, for heaven's sake. Susan, stop it!"

"You want to see him. I heard it in your voice."

"The expert!" Cathy tried to laugh and wondered what Susan would say if she told her about Robbie.

"You shouldn't be so protective, kiddo. I know you didn't ask for my advice, but since when did that stop me?" Susan chuckled softly, then went on earnestly, "You don't give yourself a chance where men are concerned. Now don't deny it. My golly, if you're intrigued by somebody, run with it. You know, run for the goal!" Susan broke off and thought a moment. "It isn't Mike, is it?"

Cathy shook her head. "I'd tell you if there was anything to tell. I'm afraid this time your romantic sleuthing is way off base."

"Think about the offer on the farm," Susan said, accepting two cookies on her way out. "Just consider it, okay?"

Cathy nodded and waved her off. She had no intention of considering the offer, and Susan probably knew it. Someone would have to be crazy to offer that much money for her crumbling-down old place. Suddenly Cathy was too exhausted to continue. She trudged back upstairs and, still in her clothes, stretched out on the bed. She set the alarm for six and fell asleep within minutes.

When the alarm rang she got up, stripped off her clothes, and stepped under a tepid shower to sponge off the day's grime. She hummed to herself as she smoothed a rich lotion over her body, then she slipped into her favorite cranberry velour robe, and padded downstairs into the kitchen to rustle up supper.

It felt strange and a bit lonely being in the kitchen by herself. She rarely had evenings alone like this and usually relished them, but for some reason tonight, watching the rosy sunset turn to violet through the window above her kitchen sink, she felt sad.

She thought of Marilyn. Usually thoughts of her oldest daughter made her smile and feel proud but tonight she imagined Marilyn cavorting on Florida beaches with her young friends and felt uneasy. Marilyn was letting herself go, having fun, frolicking and taking advantage of everything that life had to offer. Susan and Ted did zany, crazy things, too. But what about herself?

She moved to the bar in the dining room and poured herself a small glass of sherry. How long had it been since she'd had a vacation? She smiled. Never, unless she counted the harried trips she'd taken with four children to her mother's in Indiana. Last year Marilyn had offered to stay home with Amy for an entire month so that Cathy could take advantage of a group tour to Europe, but she had declined. There were always lots of reasons why she couldn't go.

She pulled out a cookbook and leafed listlessly through its sticky, dog-eared pages. Sharing a champagne breakfast with a handsome twenty-five-year-old, and then kissing him goodbye, had been the closest she'd ever come to being abandoned, to doing something unpredictable, just because she wanted to. And she had wanted to. She wanted more.

"What should I do?" she asked herself aloud as she

began putting together the ingredients for a cheese omelet. Eggs, milk, cheese, chives. She watched the butter sizzle in the skillet, hardly seeing it, then added some leftover green pepper and onion. She could always phone him.

The idea sent her into a tailspin. Her sluggishness vanished as if by magic, and she zipped around the kitchen, adding ingredients, improvising, improving, creating. She whipped the egg mixture with a flourish.

She noticed a car coming up the drive and set the mixture aside to run to the window to see who it was. It was the old Dart, choking and sputtering with its old verve. She dashed into the living room to find her checkbook. She would have to drive the mechanic back to the garage. She dashed upstairs to change, but there was a loud knock at her door so she ran back to the kitchen. The man could wait for her inside.

But it wasn't the mechanic. It was Robbie.

- 4 -

HE WAS DRESSED in brown corduroy trousers and over a white shirt he wore a sweater vest with a multicolored design on a soft beige background. His shoes were brown, and he was carrying a tan leather jacket. He looked at her calmly, without smiling, and then held out her car keys.

"I guess I should have called." He seemed subdued. "They said they weren't going to be able to get to your car until Monday, and since I knew you needed it, I didn't think you'd mind if I did the work myself."

"You did the work yourself?" Cathy echoed, staring at him.

"I worked at a garage one summer," he explained. "My dad was scared to death I'd become a garage mechanic. As if that was the worst thing that could happen to me. It was one of the best summers of my life."

"Come in." Cathy smiled tentatively and stood aside for him to enter. The aroma from the sizzling skillet permeated the kitchen, and she smiled as he sniffed the air and glanced toward the stove.

"Would you like to stay for supper?" she asked without thinking. When he turned to her with an astonished expression, she laughed. "I can see you're hungry."

"I really just finished with your car. I didn't come—"

"I know." Cathy moved to the stove and stirred the eggs. He pulled one of the heavy old chairs out from the table, and when she turned around, he was sitting down, his long legs stretched out in front of him. He was watching her. She flushed and went to the freezer to remove a loaf of bread.

"Nice kitchen." Robbie's low voice seemed to resonate through her body, stirring the erotic sensations she had been struggling against all day. Suddenly she was acutely aware of her nakedness beneath the velour robe. As she set the table, her awareness of her own body—her bare thighs brushing against each other, her arm moving back and forth as she placed the silverware on the blue and white mats—was heightened by his presence. Each time she moved closer to him, her body was seized by a longing so intense yet so deliciously pleasurable that she felt as though her feet had left the solid floor.

"Can I help?" She felt Robbie's eyes following her as if every gesture she made was the most fascinating he had ever seen. He watched her fold blue paisley napkins and tuck them under the forks. He complimented her on the wide-planked floor, which was worn and stained, and he approved heartily of the rustic ambience of the open shelves and functional gas stove. Mostly he approved of the big, old round oak table which dominated her kitchen. He ran his hand over the surface and said it was a table for laughing and telling stories at, for serious discussions late at night. Cathy glowed at his appreciation and went about making dinner with a suppressed excitement.

"Dinner's not anything special." She tossed him a

smile as she added three more eggs to the omelet mixture.

He didn't reply, but his smile told her he was content to be there. A comfortable silence fell as she moved about the kitchen. She sensed that he liked her house, and when he asked if she could hold off cooking the omelet so they could take a walk, she wasn't surprised.

She ran upstairs and put on some old clothes and returned to find him wandering around the living room. He was holding a picture of her four children that had been taken when Amy was only a year old. Marilyn had been just ten at the time. Cathy stared at the back of Robbie's broad shoulders and wondered what he was thinking.

A woman with four children? Surely the thought was a frightening one for a twenty-five-year-old man. Cathy watched as he replaced the picture on the table and picked up another, smaller, one of her and the two girls that had been taken only four months ago, just last Christmas, when Marilyn was home from college. Well, now he knew.

Cathy disguised her nervousness by remarking that they only had a few minutes to walk around before it would be too dark to see anything. Once outside, she felt better. She breathed deeply of the cool air, and they chatted casually about how warm it had been. Robbie asked Cathy about the house and its history, about her garden and the work she was doing on the guest house. He enthused over the old barn and said it was a shame it wasn't filled with livestock. His genuine enthusiasm for the farm touched her, and she could tell from his easy gait and the intensity of his expression when she explained various details that he felt at home there.

He made no move to touch her. They walked side by side, marveling at how the daffodils had come into bloom so suddenly, noting that the moon was waxing, not waning. Before going back inside, they walked into the front yard so that Robbie could admire the original section of the old brick farmhouse with its ironwork lattice and architectural detail on the roof.

Had the pictures of her family cooled his interest? Cathy wondered. Back inside they continued to converse easily as she completed the dinner preparations. As she moved to sit down, he stood up and held her chair. She thought she felt his lips brush lightly over the top of her head. The relief that flooded through her at his touch shocked and terrified her. It confirmed once again how badly she wanted him, how badly she wanted him to want her in return.

They ate slowly, speaking infrequently of irrelevant matters, and when they finished Cathy felt the old panic edging in on her. Now what? He was here with no car. They were alone. She should suggest something, take control of the situation instead of acting so ambivalently.

He insisted on helping her with the dishes. She knew she should decline. She should insist right then that she drive him back to town. But she kept silent as he took up a dishtowel.

"Why are you nervous?" he asked as he finished drying the last plate.

Cathy started to protest, then shook her head. She had learned already that there was very little she could hide from Robbie. She gave him a shaky smile and suggested that they go into the living room for a brandy.

"Almost cold enough for a fire," he said, sitting down next to her on the blue sofa.

"No wood." Cathy smiled wryly. All they needed was a roaring fire and brandy and that would be that. Good grief, she'd known him less than a day. Only it didn't feel that way. It felt as if she'd known him forever.

He slipped his fingers through hers and, with his usual candor, asked about her children. Cathy answered hesitantly at first. Then, without really noticing, she found herself telling him about the ten years since her divorce, then reaching even further back to that painful time when she first realized her marriage to Jed was over.

Robbie's smooth brow grew furrowed with concern as she shared her life's story. He shook his head and traced his forefinger along her cheek, and his expression was so pained that she smiled.

"Believe me," she assured him, "I no longer feel what you're feeling. As a matter of fact, even back then I had so much on my mind—a new baby, Marilyn, a house—that I couldn't take the time to suffer. I . . . I usually don't talk this much about it," she added.

"I asked, didn't I?" Robbie took her other hand in his and smiled. He glanced at the clock on the mantel. "It's tomorrow," he said. "We've known each other a day."

Cathy caught his meaning and laughed. "And it's time I drove you into town."

"Two o'clock is too late for you to go out." He pulled her against him, and she nestled against his broad chest. "I promise I'll go," he murmured warmly into her ear, "but I won't always go. I can't get enough of you, Cathy. I don't think I ever will."

His kiss was restrained, his mouth warm and intoxicating from the brandy. Skillfully he probed her yielding mouth. His hands moved to her shoulder and guided her down onto the sofa. She felt his passion building and made a halfhearted gesture to right herself, but her arms were around him, caressing the small of his back, his fine muscles. The pleasure of renewed acquaintance with his body heightened her desire. He twisted on top of her, and she gasped with pleasure as his weight pressed into her. His tongue filling her mouth made it impossible to think.

"Robbie." Cathy murmured his name as he showered kisses on her throat and caressed her breasts.

"Do you know what you do to me?" His voice was hoarse.

"I think so." She swallowed and fought against the fires he had ignited. She rolled over onto her side and gasped for air. "You promised..."

"I know." He seemed mesmerized by the sight of his hand covering her breast. He moved his fingers gently and, through the thin material of her blouse, began to massage her hardened nipple. He closed his eyes, smiling dreamily. "You don't wear a bra," he murmured.

In spite of herself Cathy surrendered to the delicious sensations his searching hands aroused in her. She pressed her legs into his thighs until she sensed that he was on the brink of losing control. He gathered her up in his arms again and kissed her with a ferociousness that stole her breath away.

In her heart she knew that making love was an act of trust. Was she ready for that? Robbie's body moved rhythmically against hers. If he could arouse her so with his kisses, with the sensation of his fully clothed body against her, what would happen if she gave herself to him? Her passionate response frightened her. Maybe this was how it always was with him, but never with her. In a single day her life seemed to have changed forever. She was still reeling from the shock.

He had his whole life in front of him; he was just beginning. She was bound to get burned, bound to be hurt. It would be worse than with Jed.

"I can't!" Cathy pulled away from him, and tears spilled from her eyes. "I'm sorry. It's my fault."

"It's no one's fault," Robbie soothed her.

Cathy blinked back the tears to look at him. He was still breathing heavily, still deeply aroused, yet he was more concerned about her than anything else.

"It's okay." He smoothed the top of her head and kissed her lightly on the tip of her nose as he brushed away her tears. "We have plenty of time."

"I've never had a day like today," Cathy said with effort, struggling for control.

"I haven't either." Robbie turned her around and began to massage the back of her neck until she felt the tension drain away.

"Shall I drive you back into town?" she asked hopefully, but he shook his head.

"I need a walk."

"But it's so far . . ."

"I *really* need a walk." He stood up slowly and stretched.

Cathy slipped her arm through his as she walked

him to the door. When she raised her chin for his kiss, she could see that he was still struggling for control. She placed a chaste kiss on his cheek, and he gave her one last searching look before striding out into the cool April night.

- 5 -

THREE DAYS WENT by without a word from Robbie, and Cathy felt the bittersweet ache he had aroused in her wither into a tight knot of resignation. She found herself straining to hear the phone ring and began to resent him for having drawn her out with his apparent sensitivity, only to shut her off completely.

By the third day she had sunk so low that she resorted to spending an entire morning in the beauty salon having her straight hair styled and permed into a soft body wave.

The result was flattering, but it didn't help her forget Robbie. She couldn't get him out of her mind. All the activities she used to enjoy now felt like chores. Even picking out the wallpaper for the guest house wracked her with indecision. In addition, Susan Wilcox phoned with a higher offer on the farm, and the head of the English Department called quite unexpectedly to say that he needed to speak with her. Cathy was tempted to run away from her responsibilities.

At Larrick's Hardware, Cathy sat surrounded by swatches and samples. The French provincial pattern she had previously decided on now seemed too tame. In fact all of her past choices seemed dull. But she had to make a decision today.

"I'll have that." She gestured toward a red and white contemporary design that was altogether different from her original selection. She drummed her fingers on the counter while waiting for her package. On the way out of Larrick's she was intercepted by Mike O'Sullivan, and for a moment his sunny smile lifted her spirits.

"Are we on for tonight at Susan and Ted's?" Mike leaned on a parking meter and looked admiringly at her. "Hey, I like the hair."

Cathy's hand went tentatively to her new curls. "Really?"

He nodded. "Can I buy you lunch?"

Cathy glanced at her watch. She felt a new fondness toward Mike that she hadn't felt since the early days of their dating, nearly a year ago.

She caught herself. Wasn't that what was meant by "on the rebound"? The last thing she wanted was to use Mike O'Sullivan to help soothe her disappointment over Robbie.

"I have an appointment with Dr. Bradley," she said as Mike helped put her packages in the trunk of the Dart.

"I thought this was spring vacation." Mike placed his hand on her shoulder in a friendly gesture.

"Me too," Cathy answered, and for the first time she was aware of a feeling of apprehension. Why would the head of the department phone her now? Waving goodbye to Mike, she hurried down the street toward the old stone pillars that marked the entrance to Orange College campus and blanched when she spotted Robbie leaning against a pillar watching her. She had to resist an impulse to turn around and run.

"Hello." She greeted him curtly and was surprised when he fell into stride beside her.

"Is that your boyfriend, the coach?" His tone was

caustic, but Cathy ignored it. "How's the decorating coming along?" he added when she didn't answer.

"All right." She looked straight ahead, her fury mounting. Why didn't he just go away? How long had he been standing there watching her and Mike? Why did it matter to him if she spoke to an old friend?

She glanced at Robbie's magnificent profile and felt herself soften. The veins on his neck were tight with tension, and he was holding his broad shoulders locked into position, as if ready for battle.

He hadn't said anything about her hair. He probably hadn't even noticed.

"I wanted to phone you," he said abruptly as they approached the ivy-covered building that housed the English Department.

Cathy gave him a skeptical glance and quickened her pace. He grabbed her arm and stopped her.

"I did try . . . just this morning." His pale blue eyes were filled with torment.

"I don't need this," she snapped cruelly. "I don't—"

"Let me at least explain." He drew her off the walk and over to a large maple tree that was just beginning to show traces of pale green leaves on its gnarled limbs.

"Look"—Cathy summoned up all the dignity and control she could muster—"there really isn't anything to explain. I told you it wouldn't be appropriate for us to see each other. But you can't expect me to sit home twiddling my thumbs."

"I didn't say that," Robbie broke in with an exasperated wave of his hand.

"And yes, the man you saw me with on the street

is a *good* friend of mine, though it's none of your business. You see, I'm not some languishing female who is so desperate she—"

"Now look," Robbie interrupted, raising his voice. His blue eyes pierced her. "That isn't at all what I think of you and you know it. Why can't you do me the favor of listening? You think *I'm* young. Do you realize how you're behaving?"

"Oh, listen to him." Cathy tried to laugh him off.

"Good Lord, didn't any of the time we spent together mean anything to you?" Robbie moved impatiently away from her. He looked as if he wanted to hit a tree.

Cathy gaped at him. He spoke of their time together as if it had been of some vast duration. Didn't that prove just how young and immature he was? What did he know about time?

"I have a lot on my mind today," she snapped.

"I do too!" he shouted. "Damn it!" he cried after her as she marched past him and disappeared into the office building.

All the way up the creaking stairs to the third floor she muttered under her breath. When had she been so angry? Even her anger angered her. How had she stooped so low as to stand around bickering with a child? He was right about that. She had lowered herself to his level. She should have been politely firm, certain of her position, and above being riled.

"Cathy, come on in please." Dr. Bradley, the head of the English Department, shook her hand warmly and ushered her into his book-lined office. "Some weather we're having, isn't it?" He smiled and gestured for her to sit down.

"I put in my peas yesterday." Cathy's voice was casual. She hoped she appeared as confident and controlled as always.

"I like your new hairstyle," Dr. Bradley commented. He was a white-haired gentleman in his late sixties, with a gentle way of flattering women. "Cathy," he continued, "I have an unpleasant task to do. You know that almost every college across the country is experiencing financial strain because of government cutbacks. Orange College has been hit pretty hard. The English Department has to tighten its belt along with everyone else, and what that means—much as I hate to say it—is that those instructors who have been with us for the shortest time will not be teaching as many classes next term."

Cathy sat stock still, her hands resting lightly in her lap. Of course she had known that universities everywhere were experiencing cutbacks, but somehow she had imagined herself to be immune from the possibility.

"Believe me, Cathy, it is strictly a question of seniority," Dr. Bradley offered sympathetically.

She shook her head in mute disbelief. This changed everything . . . all of her plans for the farm. Everything would change now that she wouldn't be working full-time. It had been difficult enough to make ends meet with a full teaching load, but without it . . .

"I wish I could say something to make it better." Dr. Bradley moved to her side and placed a hand on her shoulder.

"I should have been prepared," she said tightly. Suddenly she was irritated with herself for being so naive that she hadn't even considered the possibility of losing her job. Now she had already invested a significant amount of money in renovating the guest house, but she wouldn't be able to rent it unless she invested still more money.

"I know how much you love teaching," Dr. Bradley went on, "and the truth is there are several others in the department whom I would prefer to see less of. But my hands are tied."

"I know." Cathy tried to smile. For the first time since immediately following her divorce she felt the nauseating fear of financial insecurity.

Dr. Bradley's voice droned on. He would do his best to channel any outside work in her direction. He would recommend her for special tutoring. Yes, he would do everything he could to make things easier for her.

Cathy was too overwhelmed by a sense of injustice and helplessness to make things easier on Dr. Bradley. It was all she could do to maintain her composure in the face of his benevolence. When she finally stepped outside his office, she felt tears spring to her eyes.

Damn! For the first time in her life she had felt really on top of the situation, and now look where she was. As she marched down the wide corridor of the Language Building, she glanced out the window. Robbie was still leaning against the maple tree waiting for her.

Damn him! Cathy's anger erupted at the thought of all the things that were going wrong in her life — Robbie, her job. What next?

As she hurried down the outside steps, Robbie came forward to intercept her.

"Cathy." He reached for her hand, but she shrugged him off, glared at him, and marched on.

"What is it?" She felt him striding along next to her. "Cathy, what is it? What's the matter?"

She clenched her fists to keep from exploding.

"Talk to me." Robbie's voice was filled with concern—a concern she didn't want, a concern she told herself she didn't need.

"Leave me alone," she hissed.

"That's the last thing you need," he said. "To be alone. That's always your answer, isn't it? Something's happened to upset you and—"

"How would you know?" She stopped walking and faced him squarely. "How do you know so much about me . . . and . . . and even if it's perfectly obvious, what makes you think you can do anything about it?"

"I'm not sure I can." Robbie's blue eyes were soft with concern. "But I'd like to try. You shot out of that building like someone had fired you from a cannon."

Cathy took in a sharp breath. "Very apt," she said with a cynical smile. "Someone did fire me."

"You lost your job!" Robbie grabbed her by the elbows and regarded her intently. For a moment his concern for her softened her resolve and subdued her anger.

"Not exactly." She pulled away from him. She felt dazed, stunned, too uncertain about everything to continue. She moved to a nearby park bench and sat down.

"What then?" Robbie was immediately by her side. When she didn't reply he stretched his long, jean-clad legs out in front of him, crossed them at the ankles, and waited. Cathy glanced surreptitiously at him, wondering how long he would endure her silence. She didn't care. She was accustomed to sorting things out for herself. The last thing she needed was a twenty-five-year-old career counselor.

She fixed her attention on a plump robin who was working diligently to extract some morsel from the ground. She felt Robbie's attention being drawn to the bird and glanced back at him to be sure. Yes, he too was studying the busy creature.

"Look." His voice was hushed. "He's got it."

Cathy watched the robin drag its minuscule prey triumphantly along the closely cropped lawn.

"I love robins." Robbie scooted closer to her in order to see the bird better.

"Yes." Cathy felt the tension in her neck loosen, though for a moment she tried to recapture her anger, to hold on to it as a protection.

"They're funny birds," Robbie continued in a whisper. "Comics. Clowns. But friendly too."

They watched the robin fly off and fell silent once again. Cathy glanced at Robbie a third time. Something in his attitude suggested that he would wait with her as long as necessary, not out of stubbornness, but because he was sincerely concerned.

For the past ten years Cathy had turned to few people for help. Her friends marveled at her decisiveness and independence. Now suddenly she found herself wanting to unburden herself to a man she scarcely knew.

Perhaps it was his willingness to wait, the patience she sensed in him, or his ability to become absorbed in the activities of a little robin. Whatever the source, she felt a renewed confidence in him, a trust. She found herself telling him about her meeting with Dr. Bradley, about the financial struggle she had had immediately following her divorce and her fear that, after so many years of hard work, she was back to where she had started.

It was easy talking to him. He nodded his understanding, and although he said very little, she knew he was absorbing what she was saying. He seemed to understand that she didn't want advice, just his presence.

"I've felt myself at a crossroads for some time." Cathy tucked her legs up under her gray wool skirt.

"Then maybe it's for the best," Robbie said after a moment's consideration.

"Don't tell me you believe that old adage." She turned to him. *"'All's for the best in this best of all possible worlds'?* That always seems like a naive rationalization for disaster to me."

Robbie nodded thoughtfully. "No, I don't believe that everything that happens is for the best. But I do believe that events that seem painful or problematic at the time have a way of propelling us forward. Growth isn't always comfortable, and I believe that the objective of life isn't money, isn't always a job or a lot of easy laughs—it's growth. At any age. So when you said you'd felt yourself at a crossroads, maybe what you were really feeling was that you were about to grow, or that you were ready to grow." Robbie studied her for a moment, then looked away.

She admitted that there was a lot of truth in his observations. She liked the fact that he hadn't come up with easy answers, hadn't simply tried to buoy her spirits or convince her that her feelings of frustration were inappropriate or unrealistic.

"I want more," she said softly. "I love my life here in Orange, but at the same time that I am satisfied— or was until Dr. Bradley's little piece of news—I'm *not* satisfied."

Robbie nodded in agreement. "I think it's absolutely possible to love where you are yet long to be someplace else. It's a good way to be, satisfied and restless at the same time. I'm enjoying this final semester of college, but I'm anxious as hell for it to be over. Part of me wants it to last; part of me wants to move on."

"And you don't feel torn by the conflict?" Cathy asked. "You don't feel caught in the middle?"

"I feel a lot of things," Robbie acknowledged, "but the rotten feelings change. Look at you. Your situation hasn't changed, but your feelings have."

"You mean I no longer look like a raving maniac?" She chuckled at the image of herself flouncing out of the Language Building, her fists clenched for battle.

"Your anger was pretty impressive." Robbie smiled.

"I was angry at myself mostly," Cathy admitted.

"I know." Robbie's eyes met hers with a meaningful look. "And me. You were mad at me too, don't forget."

"Maybe I was." Cathy felt a tremor of desire as she looked into his blue eyes. Suddenly it seemed natural to say, "I was very disappointed when you didn't call me."

"I waited to phone you"—he leaned forward with a serious expression—"because I wanted to think."

Cathy drew in a sharp breath and shifted her legs out from under her. She knew now that if she'd thought Robbie was an impulsive young man, she'd been wrong.

"I wanted to think," he continued, "because while it's absolutely truc that I couldn't care less about the difference in our ages, I wanted to be sure I could handle a woman with four children."

"Let's not talk about it," Cathy protested nervously. He was jumping so far ahead that he was making her dizzy.

"Well, *I* thought about it," he persisted. "And that's why I called you. Even if you were Mother Hubbard I'd take you on!"

Cathy started to give him a disapproving glance, then laughed instead. "Mother Hubbard? You've got it wrong, you idiot! She had a dog, not children! If you're going to quote to the English teacher, please quote correctly. You mean the old woman who lived in a shoe who had so many children she didn't know what to do!"

Robbie fell forward laughing at himself. "I guess I'm not so smart after all." He regarded her with a sheepish grin.

"I guess not!" Cathy felt a flush of pleasure. She was positively giddy, as if she had just been seized by an acute attack of spring fever. The Cathy Thomas who had stormed out of the Language Building was gone. Basking in Robbie's warm gaze, the new Cathy felt renewed energy coursing through her body. She felt alive and bubbling with optimism. Old Mother Hubbard indeed!

"Can we go to the Owl for a beer?" Robbie's arm

brushed against her as they began walking across campus.

Cathy shook her head. Even before she had learned of the teaching cutbacks, she would have been reluctant to go to the popular beer hangout with him. Now, in addition to the problem of being seen dating a student, she felt a financial constraint.

He gave her an understanding look. "Tonight then? Can we have dinner together?" His voice was husky. She looked up at him, and their eyes locked for an instant. She felt warm and protected.

"I'm afraid I already have plans." She was sincerely disappointed.

"I won't ask you to break the date because I know you won't," he grumbled.

"You're so smart," Cathy teased, then gave a little yelp as he hit her lightly on the rear end. She laughed and suddenly felt reckless, felt like breaking into a hard run so that he would chase her . . . so that he would catch her. She imagined his strong, young body wrestling her to the ground and caught her breath. Everything led to the same conclusion.

"When then?" He towered over her as she opened the door to her car. "Tomorrow night?"

Cathy felt a stab of disappointment. She didn't want to wait until tomorrow night. "Maybe I can get home early."

His face brightened, and he moved closer to her, so close that she smelled his clean, soapy scent. His blue eyes caressed her, but he made no move to touch her again. She smiled at his control. More than anything in the world she wanted to kiss him. Instead she stared at him and he at her, and she knew that anyone passing by would have to be an imbecile not to perceive the electricity that was passing between them.

"I'll call you if I get home before ten," she said, sliding into her car. "But . . . but don't wait. I mean, if you want to make other plans . . ."

"I don't." He stuck his head through the open window and his lips parted in a kiss that passed like fire through the air between them.

Usually Cathy looked forward to her evenings with Susan and Ted, but tonight she was on edge. As usual, Susan, who loved to cook as well as to eat, was late serving dinner. Also as usual, her four children intervened at a crucial moment, postponing the culinary event even further. Cathy tried to stifle her impatience but she couldn't keep from glancing several times at her watch. Only Mike, who was his usual gregarious, good-natured, but oblivious self, didn't seem to notice Cathy's restless mood.

Finally they finished eating Susan's veal stew. Finally she and Susan were alone in the kitchen doing the dishes. Suddenly even this part of the dinner party ritual was irritating to Cathy. There was always this separation between the men and the women.

Her thoughts returned to the evening Robbie had come to dinner. He had assisted as a matter of course, never once giving her the impression that he thought he was doing her a favor by helping.

"What are you upset about?" Susan asked. "Did you and Mike have a spat?"

Cathy glanced at the kitchen clock. It was nine thirty. Did she dare call Robbie from Susan's? "We're not that intimate," she said aloud.

"Not because Mike doesn't want it. Honey, you really should loosen up. I've never seen you so touchy." While Cathy gathered her self-control, Susan took advantage of the opportunity to press her case. "Cathy, the man wants to marry you. He loves you."

Cathy shook her head. "He doesn't love me. He may think he does, but that's only because I'm the most eligible woman around and Mike wants a wife. He told me he hates being single."

Susan made a face at her. "I still say something's bugging you."

Cathy shrugged and told her about the job cutback. Immediately she knew she'd made a mistake. Her financial problems only gave Susan one more reason for telling Cathy she should consider selling the farm. She listened with what she hoped was convincing placidity, but she secretly longed to leave. She felt like a caged animal and wondered why she just didn't tell Susan what was going on. Finally she faked a headache and begged off before Ted could offer her an after-dinner brandy.

She had been in the house less than a minute when the phone rang. It was Robbie. He had been phoning every five minutes since nine. Could he come out? Yes, she told him.

Cathy hung up and sat in the dark living room with a sense of fear and anticipation. She knew perfectly well what she had agreed to. Maybe she was being ridiculous, maybe she was deceiving herself, but she had never felt such excitement. Her life had been devoted to others, to being rational and thorough, capable and responsible. At this moment she felt mad.

She felt more afraid and more euphoric than ever before. The idea of lying naked in Robbie's arms brought her near to exploding. She felt like a huge, colorful firecracker poised and ready to be set off. Of course there was a risk. There always was with fire.

- 6 -

WHEN SHE HEARD the low rumble of Robbie's MG coming up her lane, Cathy moved to the window and watched him climb out of the car and stretch. He stood for a moment looking up at the starry night, then toward the house, still without moving. Cathy sensed an anticipation in his movements that matched her own. He took his time, as if he were savoring the suspense. The pale daffodils glowed in the moonlight, and he stooped down to examine one, then looked up suddenly toward the house, as if he had guessed that she was watching him.

Cathy went to the front door and opened it, feeling unaccountably shy. He must have sensed her mood, for he embraced her as soon as the door was closed. His breath was warm as he nuzzled her neck.

His hard body made her dizzy, and she seemed to float away as his mouth came down on hers, damp and eager. Standing on tiptoe, she encircled his neck, drawing him closer, closer. She drank in the sweetness of his mouth with an audacity that made him moan with pleasure. His hips were pressed tightly against her pliant curves, and she felt bathed in luscious sensations that she knew were only the prelude to their lovemaking.

They moved as one to the couch and fell there, as easily as if they had floated down upon some puffy cloud. She smoothed and caressed his blond hair as he showered her temples, cheeks, nose, and chin with light, delicious kisses.

"You see what you do to me," he uttered. "You see how it is?"

Cathy closed her eyes, the desire in his voice arousing her more fully.

"You must have known I didn't forget," he murmured, still moving his warm lips along her face. "There wasn't a moment in those three days when I wasn't thinking of you, remembering you sitting on the fender of your car by the side of the road, seeing the promises in your green eyes."

He moved his hands to her shoulders and slid them slowly down over her breasts. "I know we should go slowly. I don't want to rush through anything with you, Cathy. I made myself wait those three days. Like you, I guess I half hoped the feelings would go away. But instead I wanted you more, more in every way— your smile, your laugh, the way you think, the way you've lived your life."

Cathy was crazy with desire. She silenced him with a kiss so penetrating and fierce that they came apart gasping.

"I'm not a casual person," Robbie whispered.

"I know, I know." She ran her palms along his chest and watched him through half-lowered lids as she began to unbutton his shirt.

"You're sure, Cathy?" His voice was strained and tense. She nodded, her eyes brimming with tears.

Swiftly he rolled her over and captured her face in his hands. Cathy bared her throat to him and he kissed it softly, making her shudder with ecstasy.

She felt charged with anticipation as he pulled himself up to stare at her. There was a sense of wonder in his eyes as they drew together, kissed lightly, then pulled apart again. Under his penetrating gaze Cathy felt herself spiraling pleasantly into a land of erotic sensations. She closed her eyes and with the tips of her fingers traced the features of his face, pausing at the appealing cleft in his chin. She wanted to know everything about him, wanted every inch of his magnificent male body to become emblazoned in her mind.

She ran her tongue, pink and moist, around his full, warm lips, and he captured her mouth with a vehemence she welcomed. She accepted him hungrily, and when his large hands slipped under her body to press her more firmly against him, she arched into his embrace.

It amazed her that even his most demanding moves were couched in gentleness. The reverence with which he gazed down at her filled her with glorious confidence. She felt his giving spirit in his inquisitive hands and mouth.

"We could go upstairs," she murmured as they separated from a long, shattering kiss.

Robbie smiled and made a halfhearted attempt to rise, but at the last moment he sank to the floor and buried his head in her breasts.

Cathy lay back blissfully as his mouth moved against her. Even through the thin fabric of her silk blouse the sensation triggered waves of pleasure. Finally, seeming to find the flimsy barrier intolerable, he removed the blouse and deftly unhooked her bra. Her bared breasts prickled in the cool air for brief moments before he leaned his warm cheek against them and she fell back onto the sofa with a groan of pleasure. His mouth covered one rosy, erect nipple while his hand teased the soft, pliant skin of the other. He touched and tasted her until she grasped his head to keep from crying out. "Robbie," she murmured again and again as he caressed her ardently.

Finally she moaned deeply, and he looked up with an exultant smile. She smiled, too, as he rose to his feet and swept her up in his arms.

She nibbled his ear and directed him toward the staircase, blissfully secure in his arms, her heart pounding with desire.

"To the right." She laughed a little as she bumped her foot against the wall. The house had never seemed more hers. She had never felt so much at home. Robbie's steps were sure and firm, his arms locked tightly around her as if they were beginning a long journey together, one that would last forever.

Her bedroom was dark and Cathy directed Robbie to the bed. He stopped when he reached it, but continued to hold her in his strong arms, as though unwilling to let her go for even an instant. Cathy felt that time must have stopped, that even the world had vanished, leaving only Robbie, herself, and her sweet, aching desire.

Then Robbie's mouth was on hers, first gently exploring then anxiously possessing. Cathy tightened her arms about his neck, and he slowly lowered her onto the bed, joining her in a fluid motion. She pressed ardently against his firm body, murmuring his name as his lips caressed her face, then complaining inarticulately when he shifted away from her.

"We're just a little too warmly dressed for this," Robbie whispered, dropping a kiss on her lips as he shrugged off his shirt.

Without hesitation Cathy helped him remove his pants, allowing her hands to trail along his long, well-muscled legs. Robbie eased her onto her back, and even in the dim light she could see his reckless grin. His hands were behind her, unhooking and unzipping her skirt, quickly pulling it off. Then he slid her pantyhose and panties over her hips and down her legs, his lips following, leaving kisses that scorched her sensitive skin.

At first Cathy shivered in the night air, then her body filled with an incredible heat that she'd never felt before. As Robbie's hands stroked her receptive body, her mind seemed hazy, as though she were feverish.

Yes, she thought as she reached for Robbie and urged him to cover her eager body with his own. She was feverish, filled with the spring fever that had intoxicated her when she had first met him—only a few days ago. Every place Robbie was touching flamed with desire; every time he kissed her, the fever gripped her more.

Cathy's hands roamed over Robbie's strong back, her lips tasted his face, his throat, any part of him within reach. She wanted to touch all of him at once, to have all of him, and she cried out her need for him.

His body pressed against hers and his lips found hers, his hot tongue fervently thrusting into her mouth.

The fever coursed through Cathy's body and she brushed her hips provocatively against his, enticing him to join with her.

He responded instantly, raising himself on his elbows as he eased his lower body onto hers, slowly forcing her thighs apart. Cathy tightened her arms about his back, gasping as her body rose to a fever pitch. She thrust her hips upward and Robbie entered her easily with a groan of satisfaction, then held himself still.

The haze covering Cathy's mind vanished and she gazed into Robbie's eyes, dark in the dark room. She caressed his cheek with a trembling hand, then smiled. If this was all just a delirious dream from her spring fever, she wanted never to be cured.

As if interpreting the smile as a signal, Robbie slowly began to move his hips. Just as slowly Cathy caught his rhythm and responded. She was aware that he was whispering something in her ear, but she couldn't pay attention. She was concentrating on the force building inside her, on the heat that was spreading throughout her, enveloping her, fusing her body with his until she didn't know where hers ended and his began, whose voice was crying out, whether it was her pleasure she felt or his—or both of theirs.

The heat of their desire, fueled by their exquisite lovemaking, was enwrapping her—both of them— in a swirling vortex until she felt herself reach the apex of her desire, until her passion had been spent and the fever broken.

Robbie nestled his head against her shoulder, sighing. She tightened her arms about him, not daring to think, to speak, wanting only to hold on, for the last few moments, to that rapturous fever that had engulfed her.

The next morning Cathy awakened to the majestic strains of Beethoven's Sixth Symphony blaring through the house. Sunlight streamed in through her bedroom window, and she noted, smiling as she rolled over on her side, that Robbie had opened the window wide to let in the fragrant spring air.

She stretched her naked limbs languidly beneath the familiar quilt. She had slept under this quilt for years, yet this morning its beauty astounded her. She picked up a corner and studied it intently then, rolling onto her back. She glanced around her room. Had she ever felt so supremely content?

She touched her lips lightly with one hand as if to feel traces of last night's passion, of Robbie's endless kisses. She chuckled and snuggled down under the covers. Was that bacon she smelled?

She closed her eyes and sniffed. It was! She could just picture Robbie nosing about her kitchen. No doubt he had already discovered the remaining jar of apricot jam and devoured some of it at least. He had probably investigated her pantry so thoroughly that he now had a complete understanding of her eating habits. He would leave no stone unturned. She was willing to wager he'd even gone through her medicine chest. The thought only endeared him to her further.

Just as she was about to hop out of bed, she heard him coming up the stairs. "Don't you dare get up!" he called. Moments later he appeared in the doorway carrying a tray laden with toast, juice, and omelets.

"You found the apricot jam," she teased as he placed the tray next to her.

Robbie licked his lips. "There's only a little left."

"Figures." She smiled as he kissed the top of her head. "No one has ever brought me breakfast in bed before."

Robbie caressed her shoulder and propped himself up next to her. He was fully clothed except for his bare feet. "This is just the beginning." He handed her a glass of juice. "I'm going to spoil you, become your slave!"

Cathy giggled as he bowed his head deferentially. "You're not convincing," she told him.

"Wait till you see what I'm planning for dinner," he said, digging into his omelet with gusto.

"Dinner!" Cathy opened her eyes wider. "Don't you think of anything but food?"

"Yes." Robbie shot her a suggestive glance, and her naked body tingled beneath the thin sheet.

She savored the omelet with an amused smile. "You're a good cook."

"You seem surprised." He nudged her playfully. "That will teach you to jump to conclusions about me. Just to whet your appetite, this evening's repast will consist of borscht, chicken Kiev, and a delectable surprise for dessert!"

She laughed with delight and kissed apricot jam from his lips.

During the rest of the week they fell into a routine that was the closest thing to heaven Cathy could imagine. Robbie rose early—it astonished her that he thrived on less than six hours of sleep—and fixed breakfast, awakening her around eight thirty with a warm kiss, which generally led to other pleasures. After a breakfast filled with laughter, Robbie would help her with one of her renovation jobs, then disappear around noon to work in the library on a research paper for his economics course. Cathy spent her afternoons happily occupied on a project, eagerly awaiting the sound of Robbie's car returning to her driveway. Their evenings varied, but given the choice, Robbie seemed to prefer spending the twilight hours wandering with her through the woods. Then the two of them would prepare an exotic meal, which meant that they didn't sit down to dinner until ten o'clock, and then there were the long, wonderful nights.

Cathy lived in a state of blissful suspension where time and the future held no power over her. It was enough to bask in the compelling and powerful warmth, humor, and passion that they shared. For the moment even her job cutback seemed an insignificant consideration in her life. She plunged ahead with the renovations on the guest house as optimistically as if nothing had changed.

Of course she knew this idyllic time couldn't last forever, but her days and nights were so perfectly filled that she didn't pause to question. When she was alone with Robbie the obstacles to their growing love seemed to vanish, including the one that was first and foremost, the difference in their ages. As for the taboo on student-professor relationships, well, when she thought about it, she realized that while she and Robbie would have to be careful in public places so as not to risk her job, it simply was not an issue between them.

Over the course of the week friends called inviting her here and there and inquiring after her whereabouts. Cathy was circumspect, but she wasn't ready to divulge her precious secret. Someday very soon she would mention Robbie to Susan, though she hadn't considered how to broach the subject. Soon, too, Amy would be coming home. But that was also something she wasn't ready to face.

When Susan's station wagon bumped up the driveway early Saturday morning, Cathy felt a flutter of apprehension, as if the enemy were about to invade her hard-won privacy. Ridiculous! she admonished herself, pulling off the red bandana she had tied around her head. It was silly to think of her best friend as her enemy. She folded up her ladder and rtan to greet Susan. Even so, she was relieved that Robbie was spending the morning in the library.

"Stranger!" Susan was dressed in a smart brown suit and heels and Cathy surmised she had spent the morning in the real estate office.

"I know." She blushed. She hadn't seen her friend since the night she and Mike had gone to Susan and Ted's for dinner. "I've been taking advantage of the peace and quiet."

"You're scraping the porch." Susan scrutinized Cathy's work. "I thought you were going to spend all your time on the guest house."

"It's almost finished." Cathy sat down on a porch step and leaned up against a pillar. The unseasonably warm temperatures had brought her flowers to an early bloom. The side garden was a profusion of delicate pastel-colored tulips.

"My goodness!" Susan exclaimed as she settled onto her favorite spot on the porch swing. "You must have been working day and night."

Cathy couldn't resist a knowing smile. "I've been busy!"

"I should say so!" Susan rolled her eyes. "You kill me. I have one measly red tulip in bloom. Lord knows how I'll get myself under control by tonight. You didn't forget tonight, did you?"

"Oh, no!" Cathy smiled enthusiastically, but she had forgotten all about Susan's party. Tonight was her big spring extravaganza. Every year she and Ted threw an enormous buffet cocktail party complete with musicians and dancing—the works. Ted was Orange College's dean of students, and the party was primarily for members of the faculty, although Susan made a point of including "new blood," as she referred to her out-of-town guests.

A look of suspicion crossed Susan's face as she studied Cathy. "You did forget."

"I didn't!" Cathy laughed her protestation. Susan would have been broken hearted to think that the big event had slipped her mind. "I even bought a new dress." Well, it hadn't been specifically for Susan's party, she amended silently, but it was new and would suit just fine.

Susan smiled and launched into a description of a new recipe for pâté. "I should go home"—she sighed— "but I hired someone to clean. Ted insisted. Do you believe it? *He* insisted. I argued that we couldn't afford it, what with hiring the musicians and all—we're having five this year instead of three—but he insisted, so I went into the office this morning, and here I am like a lady of leisure."

Cathy's smile froze as she heard Robbie's MG turn into the lane. She glanced quickly at her watch. It was only eleven. Her heart was racing. What would he do when he saw Susan? She felt cornered and unprepared. She should have told Susan before. Told her about what? About her . . . affair. It was an affair, wasn't it?

Time seemed to stand still. Susan droned on about something to do with the party as Robbie parked. "You have company," Susan said finally, watching as Robbie opened the trunk of his car.

Cathy felt paralyzed. Susan's next question was bound to be, Who is it? What would she say then?

Gripped by what she knew was a very foolish and probably unnecessary terror, Cathy rose stiffly to her feet. Susan didn't have a prudish bone in her body. What in the world was she afraid of?

Robbie advanced toward them, wearing faded jeans, tennis shoes, and a snug blue T-shirt that said SAVE THE WHALES. He was carrying a box of pansies. Cathy pounced on the detail like a seasoned detective.

"Oh good, you brought them!" She ran forward to meet him and gave him a warning glance. He looked amused but nodded.

Cathy turned and marched back to Susan. "Susan, this is a friend of mine, Robbie Darrow. Robbie, this is Susan Wilcox. Her husband's—"

"Ah, the dean," Robbie filled in as he placed the pansies on the porch, wiped his hand on his jeans, and offered it to Susan, who shook it vigorously.

"I've seen you before," Susan said, studying him.

"He's a student," Cathy rushed in.

"Of course." Susan stood up.

"Where would you like these planted?" Robbie turned to Cathy and then, to her horror, added, "Mrs. Thomas?" She could have killed him for that.

She cast him a scathing look. She felt like a dope. Why couldn't she behave normally? Why did she feel so panicked?

Before she could reply and, again to her utter horror, she heard Susan inviting him to her party.

"That's very nice of you." Robbie folded his arms in front of the whale logo and smiled. Susan smiled smugly, as if she had just struck gold. So Robbie was going to be some of the "new blood" at her party, was he? Knowing Susan, Cathy figured she had an ulterior motive, which no doubt concerned matching Robbie up with...

Cathy forced her attention back to Susan and Robbie, who were chatting casually about the increase in land values around Orange.

"Good grief!" Susan whirled on Cathy. "I almost forgot. There's been another offer on the farm." Cathy tried to look interested. "Cathy, we have to talk about this," Susan went on, her voice all business. "Monday. Honey, let's have lunch on Monday and discuss it then."

Cathy nodded. She'd agree to anything to be rid of Susan. Suddenly she felt pressured. Her secret world had been irretrievably invaded.

"Why don't you and Mike come early," Susan called over her shoulder as she headed toward her car. Robbie cast Cathy a sly grin, but she was not amused.

"He's off visiting his kids," she called. Thank God for small favors. At least Mike wouldn't be hovering around her, making her even more uneasy than she was likely to be anyway. How she dreaded the evening ahead!

As soon as Susan had left, Cathy picked up the trowel and began digging furiously along the side of the porch. She felt Robbie standing over her.

"What the hell was that all about?" he asked.

Cathy placed a pansy in the hole and pounded the dirt down around it. "I didn't know what to say to Susan about you." Ashamed of herself, she couldn't meet his gaze.

"Why did you think you had to say anything?" He crouched down beside her. Ignoring him, she continued planting pansies.

"Cathy . . ." He touched her arm, but she jerked it away. Finally she stood up.

Robbie fell back onto the grass and shook his head. "I don't get it. I arrive with a box of pansies and I'm greeted by a frenetic woman, like something from a spy novel. Only who was the spy? Me?"

"You don't understand," Cathy began, feeling helplessly confused. "Don't you see that with the cutbacks it's dangerous for me to be seen going out with you? I can't risk any gossip. Not that Susan would— oh damn!"

Robbie frowned with concern. "I do understand and I think I performed admirably."

"Okay, you did. You—"

"Didn't let the cat out of the bag," he filled in, a cynical note in his voice.

Why was he carrying on like this? She already knew she'd behaved like an idiot.

"I don't know." Robbie stood up and kicked at the grass. "It seems to me you're all turned around about this. If I were some guy your own age, someone you *think* would be a more suitable . . . consort, would you have said, 'Oh, Susan, here's Rod Tom Ralph, the man I'm sleeping with'?"

"Of course not!" Cathy snapped. "Don't be foolish."

"Me foolish?" Robbie shook his head angrily. "You were acting as if you were ashamed of me!"

"Look, I think you know how I feel. It doesn't mean anything to us, but student-professor relationships are frowned on and I feel really vulnerable right now. What if some disagreeable person found out about us and decided to use it against me? I'd be out of a job completely. Don't you understand?" Cathy squinted up at him.

His blond hair was tousled, his blue shirt stretched appealingly over his broad shoulders. She closed her eyes and shook her head. "Of course I'm not ashamed of you," she added quietly. "I'm sorry, Robbie. I know it was awkward for you. Thank you for going along with my silly game."

Robbie tilted her chin up, and his eyes grew soft. "I'm a man first, a student second," he said. "I thought we'd settled that."

"I thought so too." Cathy picked up the trowel and began digging again.

"But now you're not sure?" Robbie placed the flat of pansies between them and squatted down beside her. "It seems to me that not wanting to confide in your best friend has to do with something other than university standards."

Cathy glanced briefly up at him. Very little escaped him. He refused to gloss over problems. He was perceptive and wise.

Maybe he was right now. Maybe there were other reasons to keep their arrangement secret. He had almost been living there. They had been sharing everything, and she didn't want it to end. She wanted these blissful, sun-filled spring days to go on and on.

But Susan's visit had brought her back to reality, and the reality was that she and Robbie couldn't continue as they had. Amy would be home soon, and Cathy would resume what was left of her teaching schedule. Eventually Robbie would graduate and leave Orange.

"Cathy . . ." Robbie drew her to her feet. "You're trying to protect yourself from all sorts of things that won't happen." He kissed her softly, then stood back to look at her. "I know I can't be around all the time when Amy comes home, but I don't mind. I can't wait to meet her. It's going to be all right. Trust me."

"I do trust you." Cathy met his gaze without wavering.

"If you feel uneasy about Susan's party, I'll stay here," Robbie offered. "I'll finish papering the bathroom."

"I can't let you do that," Cathy exclaimed, feeling both foolish and frustrated. "Let's just drive separately. I don't want to hide or play games, but I just can't risk—"

"I know." He pulled her close. "Hey, it's not a tragedy, and it's not going to last forever. Once I'm a bona fide Orange graduate, you can present me to society."

Cathy looked up at him with a wan smile. "Your coming-out party?"

He nodded. "Why not?"

"You're silly." Cathy stood on tiptoe to kiss him.

"That's because I love you."

The simple statement brought her up short. She stared at him, asking silently for a further explanation.

"Let's go inside," he said, his voice suddenly husky. He took her hand and led her to the back door. Cathy followed him through the cool, silent interior. Their feet echoed on the stairs, down the corridor, and into their bedroom. She caught herself up short. She had thought of the bedroom as *theirs*.

Robbie leaned down and kissed her gently. His lips were cool, but she sensed a restrained passion in him. His hands slid beneath her sweater and cupped her breasts firmly, caressing them with slow, languid movements that sent her floating away into another world.

Cathy put her arms around his neck and raised her mouth to his. She tasted his lips and teased her tongue inside his mouth, wanting to taste all of him, wanting to excite and thrill him, to bring all of his senses to glorious and throbbing life. She wanted to penetrate to his soul as he had penetrated to hers.

He had declared his love easily, so unexpectedly, that only now was she beginning to feel the full impact of his words. She felt transformed by his love, shaken to her very core, and yearned to show him through touch what she wasn't ready to say yet in words— that she loved him too.

She raised her arms as he pulled her sweater over her head, and for a moment she stared into his intense blue eyes. She was astounded by the depth of feeling she read in them. He stroked her along her torso, then moved to unsnap her jeans and draw them down over her hips. As she stepped out of them, he slid his hands beneath the flimsy panties, and she moaned with pleasure as he spread his fingers over her buttocks and pressed her against his throbbing body.

Swiftly Cathy's hands moved to his belt buckle, and moments later she felt his bare legs pressing against hers. She luxuriated in the feel of the soft hairs that curled along his legs, rubbing against her smooth thighs. His mouth covered hers in a blinding kiss that sent them tumbling onto the bed.

With a wild abandon she had come to accept as part of their lovemaking, Cathy guided his hand to where she longed to be touched. She moved restlessly against him, unable to endure the ecstasy his fingers ignited in her.

"I love you, Cathy."

The words exploded in her body as she arched against him. She felt him shudder as her knowing fingers drove him to greater heights. He removed the last barrier between them and then joined with her, filling her mind, body, and soul with his fiery young spirit.

She had never seen him so ardent, so intent on arousing her to the point of madness. He held himself on the brink when time after time her body shuddered its gratitude as waves of pleasure undulated through her. Then he slowed and his movements became con-trolled and deliberate until, finally driven beyond endurance, they sped to a shattering climax and lay gasping in each other's arms.

Moments later Robbie rolled to Cathy's side and drew her up against his strong, naked body. They lay on their backs, holding hands as the mild spring air dried their damp bodies. Cathy glanced at him and saw that he was regarding her pensively.

"I love you." His blue eyes were luminous, his voice as gentle as the breeze.

There was a knot in Cathy's throat as she smoothed her hand tenderly across his damp forehead. "I love you too," she said simply.

- 7 -

CATHY PARKED THE Dart in front of Susan and Ted Wilcox's sprawling split-level house, which was located near the homes of many faculty members in an elite section of town. As she slammed the car door closed, she spotted Robbie's green MG parked near the corner.

She cut through the yard in her strappy high-heeled sandals, feeling both sexy and sophisticated. She'd worn her new two-piece melon-colored outfit. The softly pleated silk skirt clung to her body, accentuating her small waist, and the top, a bit risqué for her, left one shoulder bare.

Cathy was anxious to see Robbie's reaction to the outfit. He had never seen her dressed up before and, with the elegant pearl-drop earrings and new dress, she was as dressed up as she'd been in ten years. The thought made her chuckle.

She paused to consider Susan's dwarf tulips before walking toward the deck at the back of the house, from where she could hear the faint strains of music.

"Hey, throw that to me, Robbie!" Cathy recognized the excited voice of Susan's nine-year-old son, Larry. She turned in time to see Robbie, elegantly attired in a dark-brown suit with a white shirt and tie, heaving a football at the youngster in the side yard.

Larry caught the ball and charged toward Robbie, who wrestled him gently to the ground.

"Me too, Robbie. Take it away from Larry and give me a chance too!" cried Sara, Susan's competitive six-year-old.

"Okay, Sara." Robbie moved closer to the tiny, dark-haired girl. The football was practically as large as she was, Cathy noted as Robbie gave Sara patient instructions on how to catch the ball.

"Wonderful!" Robbie exclaimed when she managed to keep hold of it.

"Me again, me again!" Sara ran to Robbie and hugged his knees, then stared lovingly up at him.

Cathy caught her breath as a sudden thought sent a wave of anxiety through her. Why hadn't she considered it before? Of course Robbie would want a family! Seeing him cavorting with Susan's children made her see what should have been obvious to her much sooner. Hadn't he confided in her about his disappointment and regret in his own family—in the father who was always working, in the mother he rarely saw? And he loved to hear Cathy talk about her own children.

For the first time Cathy thought she understood some of what Robbie saw in her. She represented the antithesis of his Connecticut family. She owned a comfortable, run-down farm instead of a decorator's dream mansion. She cooked, gardened, repaired things, and even sewed curtains. She had mothered four children, pursued a teaching career, and still found time to be Amy's Brownie troop leader. She was everything Robbie had longed for and never had.

She would soon be thirty-six. Her children were growing up, needed her less. She was just coming into her own, free and independent for the first time in her life. The mothering stage of her life was almost complete, and she didn't want to start over by having more children.

But Robbie would want children. He deserved them. Cathy watched him running with the little ones tagging after him. He was having a wonderful time.

She felt breathless as she went around back and climbed the steps to the deck, although she managed to convey her usual good humor and enthusiasm as she greeted people, most of whom she knew through work. She chatted with Dr. Bradley and assured him that she had recovered from the initial shock of the cutbacks. She described the renovations she was making on the farm.

But her breathlessness wouldn't go away. Why hadn't she thought of children before? Why hadn't she stuck with her original intention not to become involved with a man so much younger than herself? Now she was in deep trouble. Her heart was so full of him that the idea of losing him was actually making her ill.

Dr. Bradley and Cathy were joined by the president of Orange College, Dr. Rupert Hall, and his daughter, Lori.

"You've met Lori, haven't you, Cathy?" Dr. Hall put an arm around his daughter, a stunning young woman of about twenty with long, honey-colored hair and a shy smile.

"Of course." Cathy shook Lori's delicate hand. "You're home for spring vacation, I take it?"

Lori smiled sweetly. "As much as I love California, I still miss the changing seasons, especially spring."

"And this is an extraordinary spring." Dr. Hall

remarked with his usual exuberance. "Cathy, may I get you something to drink?"

"No thank you. I think I'll go see if Susan needs any help." Cathy made her way to the kitchen, where Susan was giving last-minute orders to three harried helpers. Cathy tossed her friend a kiss and moved into the living room, which was humming with conversation. She wanted to be alone to catch her breath and think, but that was impossible. Instead, she returned to the deck, which was filled with couples dancing, and ordered a gin and tonic from a student who was acting as bartender. Leaning against the deck railing, she looked off into the yard. Robbie and the children were nowhere in sight.

Monsieur Berne, the new French professor, caught her eye, and before she could stop him, he had cornered her. As usual, he had already had too much to drink and was talking and flirting outrageously, despite his wife's presence.

Finally Cathy was able to excuse herself. She headed back inside, wondering where Robbie was. Had he become bored and left early? But he wouldn't have gone off without a word, would he?

The drink eased Cathy's tension slightly, and when Ted asked her to dance, she threw herself into his arms and whirled around the deck, trying to have a good time.

"You look fabulous." Ted grinned down at her. "Has Sus seen that getup?"

"I don't think Susan's seen anything." Cathy laughed. "I don't think she really enjoys these parties until she looks at the pictures."

Ted chuckled. "You're right. She enjoys them in retrospect."

They danced a while longer, then Ted said, "Cathy, would you excuse me? The idea of Susan slaving away in the kitchen and me kicking up my heels has stirred up a bit of guilt."

"Good for you," Cathy told him as he left her. Before she could move out of the dance area, Sam Rollins, a math professor, caught her hand and she was thrown into an energetic dance as the band switched from conservative tunes to hard rock. Sam was a good dancer. Cathy lost herself in the scorching rock music and cheered along with the rest of the crowd when the band finished the number. Just then Sam's wife, Helen, joined them, giving Cathy a peck on the cheek and inquiring after Amy.

After chatting with her friends for several minutes, Cathy excused herself and headed toward Susan's bedroom to freshen up. She was carrying a fresh gin and tonic and trying not to spill it as she weaved in and out among the guests when, out of the rumble of conversation, she heard Robbie's low baritone.

She located him deep in conversation with Lori Hall. They were seated next to each other on a beige sectional, their faces earnest, their blond heads close together. Cathy's heart seemed to stop as she watched them. They made a perfect match. So that was why Susan had invited Robbie. She had seen him as the ideal escort for President Hall's daughter.

And it was true. Cathy winced as Lori leaned even closer to Robbie and said something that made him throw back his head and laugh. The sound ripped like a knife through Cathy's body, and she nearly collided with Leslie Harris, who was helping Susan pass the hors d'oeuvres tray.

To Cathy's relief, Susan's bedroom was deserted. Cathy closed the door and locked it, then sat on the edge of Susan's bed and stared into her gin and tonic. Lori Hall's fresh blond beauty wouldn't leave her mind. She knew it was stupid, but suddenly even her silk outfit felt all wrong.

No, of course thirty-six wasn't old. It especially wasn't old if your friends were in their forties and fifties. But what about Robbie? So far she hadn't even met any of his friends, but she knew they were his age or younger, like pretty Lori Hall. Damn! And she liked Lori Hall. She had known her when she was still in pigtails. Lori had graduated from Orange High School only two years ahead of Marilyn. For heaven's sake, Lori had been to slumber parties at her house!

She gulped down the gin and tonic. She was furious at herself for being concerned about Lori Hall. How ridiculous to feel in competition with one of her daughter's contemporaries. It was an impossible situation.

Cathy returned to the party with a phony smile she detested herself for wearing. Robbie and Lori were no longer on the sofa. They were probably outside dancing, Cathy surmised. She decided not to torment herself by watching their young bodies gyrate to the hard rock music. What the hell, she liked dancing to that music. She had been brought up on that music, too. It was her music, too.

She felt defensive, as if someone had accused her of something. She vowed not to have anything more to drink, and in an attempt to rise above the occasion, she loaded a plate full of Susan's delicious food and joined a group of friends.

"Hi." Just as she was finishing her dinner she felt a light tap on her bare shoulder. A rush of excitement swept over her as she turned to meet Robbie's blue eyes. "Having a good time?" he asked brightly.

She smiled and shrugged. "It's a good party."

He leaned down with a conspirator's smile. "Is it safe for us to dance?"

"Not on a full stomach," she told him with the same stiff smile, wishing he wouldn't look at her like that in front of everyone.

Robbie reached for her hand. She tried to pull away, but he held on to it, staring at her hungrily. His approval of her outfit was implicit. Cathy's body prickled with desire.

She shook his hand lightly as if he were playing a game. "You'd better get to that ham before . . ."

He drew her to her feet and she laughed. "What are you doing?" Damn him, he was steering her through the crowd back onto the deck, where the music had turned soft and slow. She said something inane in the same casual, almost patronizing tone that she thought would be convincing, but he said nothing and pulled her firmly to him. Against her will her body melted into his as they began to dance.

"You've been avoiding me." His breath was hot against her ear. "We agreed to come in separate cars. We did not agree to pretend to be strangers." He caressed her bare shoulder.

"Robbie, stop that."

"No." He caught her earlobe in his mouth, and she

felt the blood gush into her loins.

It didn't matter. She closed her eyes and allowed him to lead her. It really didn't matter now who thought what or why. She wasn't going to see him anymore. The reasons why it was an impossible romance were more complicated and more numerous than the difference in their ages.

"I want to get you home," Robbie whispered. "Your friends are very nice, but I like the silence of our room better."

What did he mean by *our* room? What sort of a line was that, and what had Lori Hall said earlier to make him throw back his head and laugh? Cathy bit her lip. That kind of thinking was beneath her. She tried to recall the euphoria she had felt earlier when he had told her he loved her. Why wasn't that enough? He loved *her*. He desired *her*, not Lori Hall. But Lori was young, and Cathy couldn't shake the traditional, ingrained logic that young women were always preferable. There would always be Lori Halls around, and she would always have doubts. Next year she would be thirty-seven, then thirty-eight, thirty-nine, and then forty.

"Come on, Cathy. Loosen up, dance with me." Robbie began massaging the tight muscles at the small of her back. They danced a few steps, then Cathy stopped. Her eyes scanned the crowd on the deck. Nobody was even looking at them.

Robbie wore a satisfied grin. "You see? Most of your worries are up there." He tapped her head lightly.

But not all, Cathy thought as she met his amused eyes. "I wish I could stop thinking," she told him candidly.

"Why? You have a fine mind. One of the best," he teased.

"I'm serious." Cathy walked over to a deserted corner of the deck. Suddenly she was seized by an urgent need to bring everything out into the open, to make him finally face the reality of how impossible their future was. She almost wanted it to end. She would feel the pain and recover. She was good at recovering. It crossed her mind vaguely that she wasn't perhaps so good at love . . . at enjoying the moment and living in the present.

He looked down at her questioningly. The words stuck in her throat. Wasn't she jumping ahead by bringing up the question of children? He had said he loved her, but to him love might not have anything to do with the future.

"I don't usually behave in this jumpy, irrational way," she said with a sad smile.

"I know you don't," he replied softly. "Maybe you've spent too much energy being an optimistic dynamo. Maybe you're just catching your breath."

"At your expense."

"Look, all I care about is that you don't close me off, that we can talk about whatever's on your mind." Robbie leaned against the deck railing.

Cathy stared out across the lawn, where he had romped with Susan's children. She wasn't saying what was on her mind. She could practically feel the rusty hinges of her mind closing tighter and tighter. After living for years keeping everything to herself, it wasn't easy to change, no matter how badly she wanted to.

"Maybe we should leave," Robbie offered. "Maybe we can discuss whatever it is better at home."

Cathy smiled ruefully. How easily he referred to the farm as *home,* as if it were his home too. "You're right," she said after a moment. "Why don't you leave first. I'll go help Susan with...whatever."

"Are you okay?" Robbie touched her elbow solicitously.

"I feel like a crybaby," she confessed.

"I don't see any tears. Stop putting yourself down. Something's on your mind. You don't have to apologize."

Cathy threw him a grateful smile as she started toward the kitchen to pay her respects to Susan.

After a reasonable time had lapsed after Robbie's departure, Cathy got into the Dart and drove off. What was she going to say? She hated confrontations. She was tempted to drive off into the night with no destination, just drive and drive until she was too tired to go on and then check into a motel someplace. Good Lord, she really had lost her mind. She had never behaved like this. Never!

She drove right past her driveway and circled aimlessly around Orange. Finally she returned home with a sense of foreboding.

Low clouds scudded across the dark sky, blocking out the stars. Cathy shut the car door and stared up at the murky sky. It would probably rain tomorrow; the fair weather was coming to an end. How appropriate. She smiled wryly.

Robbie was sitting on the swing on the back porch. The seat moved back and forth in the shadows, but he didn't say anything. Cathy swallowed hard as the memory of seeing him romp through the yard with Susan's children flooded back to her.

She approached him slowly, uncertainly. She had no idea what to say, and the silence of the night, the sense of mystery created by those low, fast-moving clouds, seemed to inhibit her words. She sat down at the far end of the swing, took off her shoes, and tucked her feet into the corner. He had fixed the squeak on the swing, she recalled. Three days ago he had insisted on taking down the entire swing and oiling and cleaning the chain before securing it again with new bolts.

He reached across the distance and took her hand. "We need rain," he said simply, seeming to imply much more.

"I know," she admitted softly.

"Don't be afraid of me."

"I'm not. I'm really not."

"I think you are," he answered softly. "I feel as if I'm on trial with you. Oh, not all the time. Not when we make love or plant the garden or even walk in the woods. But a lot of the time I feel you're looking for reasons why we shouldn't be together."

Cathy watched the clouds glide over the moon, saw the filtered moonlight spilling down onto the pansies they had planted earlier. "I saw you with Susan's children," she said after a long pause.

"They're fabulous kids."

Cathy felt her throat tighten, as if his enthusiasm for Larry and Sara was a confirmation of all of her fears. Thirty-six wasn't too old to have children. But she didn't want that. That part of her life was over.

"And what about you? Would you want children?" She had to force the words out.

"Of course!" His reply came swiftly. He looked at her curiously. Clearly he hadn't seen her underlying motive in bringing up the subject.

He tugged gently at her fingers, then raised her hand to his mouth and began kissing the tips lightly. "What is it?" His eyes pleaded with her.

"Did it ever occur to you that you and I are simply at different phases in our lives? Age aside, we're just . . ." She trailed off and looked at him helplessly.

"Like, what about children," she forced herself to say. "I have four. They're wonderful. I don't think I'd want to have more."

She couldn't bring herself to look at him. Instead she stared at the milky cloud formations. She could almost feel him thinking. No, he would never lie to appease or soothe her. His silence told her she'd been right. He had never considered the possibility that they might each want something totally different out of the future.

Cathy's eyes filled with tears, not only for herself but for him as well. In his well-meaning, loving enthusiasm it had never occurred to him that she might not be as eager for the sweetness of domestic life as he was.

"I love you." She turned to him, her eyes damp with tears.

He took her face in his hands and searched it tenderly. "Please, don't worry. Let's love each other." His powerful arms embraced her, and as his mouth sought hers, she knew that for the night at least he was hers.

- 8 -

AS SHE LAY in his arms later that night, Cathy thought how remarkable it was that his impassioned yet tender lovemaking was the antidote to all her worries. His fervent mouth moved from her breasts down to her taut stomach, where his tongue made erotic patterns across her skin.

Once again the impossible seemed not only possible but inevitable. He moved his searching hands along the sensitive skin of her inner thighs and, by carefully avoiding the source of her deepest pleasure, seemed to drive her higher and higher. He moved his hand down the bare length of her leg, testing the calf muscle. His every touch sent fire coursing through her veins, and her moans lured him onward.

The passion of their lovemaking had grown during their brief acquaintance. Cathy felt that, like a blaze to which fuel has been added, their love was now a raging fire that could not be cooled.

She gripped his shoulders and threw her neck back in exaltation as he penetrated to her very core. They were one, and their oneness arose from more than passion. They moved together in the skillful task of giving each other pleasure, and when Cathy looked at Robbie in the very heat of their lovemaking, she knew that he too felt the wonder of their coming together.

He rolled over without missing a beat, and Cathy

felt a fierce eagerness as she endeavored to bring him to even greater heights. His ecstatic gasps sent her spirit soaring and her earlier fears faded away. Surely loving each other as they did meant that nothing was impossible.

As they flung themselves together, the entire universe seemed to shatter. Cathy lay trembling on his damp and heaving chest.

"We did it," he said breathlessly.

"What?" Cathy asked in a dazed voice.

"Don't you hear the thunder? You mean my lovemaking obliterates natural phenomena?" He chuckled quietly.

Cathy smiled languidly as another crack of thunder shook the house. "I don't hear a thing," she muttered, opening her mouth against the down of hair on his chest. "I don't hear a thing."

When she awoke the next morning, she didn't remember falling asleep, but the storm that had occurred in the early hours of the morning seemed to have been part of a glorious, cleansing dream.

Robbie slept with one hand resting lightly on her breasts. His fingers were curled slightly, and he was breathing as evenly as a baby. Cathy watched his hand rise and fall with her own even breathing.

It was rare to see him asleep. She smiled as she studied his long blond lashes, his smooth eyelids, and his cheeks, which showed a stubble of beard. Perhaps he was right and love was the only thing that really mattered.

But it was too soon in the day to think. In a way she wished she could be the sort of glamorous older woman who took an egotistical pride in having a young lover. She had heard and read about such women. They always sounded so daring, so sophisticated, and entirely unlike herself. There was certainly nothing risqué about her feelings for Robbie.

Careful not to disturb Robbie, Cathy twisted to look at the clock. Nearly ten thirty! Gingerly she lifted his hand off her breasts and placed it on the sheet. She rolled to the side of the bed, and just as it seemed she had succeeded in extricating herself without waking him, he grabbed her arm.

"Where are you going?" He pulled her back into bed and regarded her with bright eyes. Cathy smiled. He was either totally awake or totally asleep, with no grogginess in between.

She leaned over and kissed his nose. "Up. I'm getting up. I'll get breakfast this morning."

"Umm." He nibbled her shoulder. Cathy felt a yearning stir and knew that with very little coaxing she would be wrapped in those strong arms once again.

Robbie threw back the sheet and looked unabashedly at her. A week ago she would have blushed and pulled the sheet back up. Now she allowed his eyes to travel over her naked curves; she relished the extent to which he could arouse her without even touching her.

"Roll over," he directed without moving his eyes from her. "On your side."

With a sense of heady unreality Cathy complied, rolling to one side facing him. His hand moved to the curve of her hip, which was greatly accentuated by her position. He ran his hand back and forth from thigh to breast, as if he were an artist contemplating some great work. When Cathy said as much, he smiled.

"Maybe I am," he teased as his fingers ran lightly along her silky flank. "Maybe I haven't told you all there is to know about me."

"I don't doubt that," she teased. "All of those skeletons in your closet. A man of many faces is what you are."

"And all of my faces love you." Suddenly he pounced on her, rolling her playfully onto her back. Just then she heard the crunch of gravel in the driveway below and bolted to a sitting position.

"Don't panic!" He shook his finger at her, still in a carefree mood.

"Who, me?" Cathy jumped out of bed, started to throw on her robe, thought better of it, and wriggled into her jeans. A glance out the window at the drippy, gray Sunday told her that Susan Wilcox, still in her church clothes, was tiptoeing through the wet grass. Cathy raced down the stairs and arrived in the kitchen just as Susan tapped at the door.

"Got some coffee?" Susan shoved a white pastry box into Cathy's hand the moment she was inside.

"Just making some." She flew to the sink and turned on the cold water. "I thought you'd sworn off of Max's doughnuts."

Susan was already seated at the kitchen table, loosening the string on the box. "Special occasion." She laughed. "The day after the night before. I'd say it was one of my best, wouldn't you?"

"It was a fabulous party. I had thirds on the ham." Cathy plugged in the electric coffeepot and tried to think of a way to keep Susan from hanging around for the next hour and a half. It was obvious that her friend had come for a long rehash of her party.

"You slept late, huh?" Susan munched blissfully on a sugar-coated doughnut. Cathy's stomach felt queasy. She hadn't even brushed her teeth.

She nodded and broke a corner off a doughnut so Susan wouldn't question her. They both adored doughnuts and frequently indulged in an after-church coffee-and-doughnut binge at Cathy's round oak table.

What was she going to tell Susan about Robbie? Cathy racked her brain, but her mind felt like mush.

"Your friend was quite the success." Susan finished her doughnut and removed her suit jacket.

"My friend?" Cathy almost choked on her doughnut.

"The cute blond, Robbie whatshisname. Everyone was very impressed with him. My kids haven't stopped talking about him. It's Robbie this, Robbie that. I think I'll invite him to dinner."

"You should!" Cathy exclaimed. "He'd love it. I don't think he knows many people around here, and I don't know for sure, but since he's older than the other students, I imagine...I imagine he's rather lonesome. At least that's the impression I get. Yes, he's nice, isn't he?"

"Lori Hall seems to think so." Susan smacked her lips and eyed another doughnut as Cathy jumped up from the table on the pretense of checking the coffee. "The young, the blond, and the beautiful," Susan went on. "Remember Lori with that mouthful of braces? I hadn't seen her since she went off to college. She's a knockout."

"Ravishing," Cathy blurted out.

"He's helping you again, I take it?" Susan inquired casually.

"Who?" Cathy was momentarily rattled. "Oh, you mean Robbie Darrow?" Good grief, she had actually forgotten that Robbie's car was parked outside. Susan knew he was there.

"Yes." Cathy poured them each a cup of coffee, relieved to see that her hand wasn't trembling. She strained to hear any sound from upstairs. Knowing Robbie, he had probably crept soundlessly downstairs and was hiding just inside the dining room door choking back his laughter.

"Yes, he's um... quite adept at fixing things. Loves to putter around. He's been a big help to me."

Cathy could continue the charade no longer. Suddenly the whole thing struck her as totally absurd. "Actually, Susan, I'm having an affair with him," she announced before she could censor herself.

Susan dropped the remainder of her doughnut, and her eyes seemed to blow up like balloons. A skeptical smile crossed her face. "You're not."

Cathy drew her lips together and nodded solemnly.

"You are?" Susan, who was never flabbergasted, who was always the bearer of news and hardly ever the receiver, was speechless.

"And you're sworn on your life to secrecy." Cathy felt an enormous sense of relief at being able to share her news with someone. She had missed talking to Susan. True, Susan was a gadfly, but Cathy was convinced that in this instance she would be discreet.

"You're... *sleeping* with him?" Susan rolled her eyes enviously. This, Cathy thought, was more like the Susan she knew—the lovable, nosy, slightly bawdy busybody who simply adored to listen to anything that had to do with sex and romance.

"Well, kiddo," Susan extended her hand to Cathy, "I got to hand it to you, I didn't have a clue. I swear, this is one time Susan Wilcox slipped up. And you of all people! Is that why you sent Amy to Jed's for the entire vacation?"

"I didn't even know Robbie until after I'd left Amy with her father," Cathy explained, leaning back in her chair. She guessed that if Robbie had been eavesdropping he would be proud of her. No doubt he'd immerse himself in a book and leave her and Susan alone. What a relief!

"You didn't even know him?" Once again Susan's eyes opened wide. "He wasn't in one of your classes? You didn't meet him that way?"

Cathy giggled. Susan had completely forgotten about the doughnuts. As Cathy related the details of the past week and a half, Susan hung on every word, nodding and smacking her lips with glee.

When Cathy had finished the story, Susan leaned across the table and whispered, "And how is he? I bet he's great! I've always dreamed of a younger man."

Cathy blushed slightly at Susan's ribald reaction. It didn't exactly surprise her, but she might have wished for a more sensitive response. Ah well, that was Susan.

"I want *all* the details." Susan looked furtively over her shoulder. "But later. Let's have lunch tomorrow. Oh, we're having lunch anyway to talk about the farm. The offer on the farm, remember? Lord, no wonder you can't think about real estate. Don't worry, Cathy,

I won't breathe a word." She lowered her voice even further. "As long as you promise to tell me *everything!*"

Cathy's smile vanished. She moved back to the coffeepot and poured them each another cup. Susan had the wrong idea.

"This is just what you need, honey, before you settle down," Susan continued, adding two heaping spoonsful of sugar to her coffee. "You need a good fling like this. He's so young! You be careful, though. You don't want this thing to leak out and ruin things with Mike. Oh, honey, I'm just thrilled for you! Mum's the word!"

"I'm in love with him, Susan." Cathy's voice was hushed.

"Now come on, kiddo, he's a baby. Don't get hung up on naming a good thing love."

"I'm not hung up at all. That's the way it is. I've never felt like this in my life." Cathy stared into the thick brown coffee. Funny how talking about Robbie and her feelings seemed to make everything less ambiguous.

"Honey, go easy. You've heard of midlife crises? You've been lonely all these years. Just lie back and accept it for what it is."

Susan's words shook Cathy momentarily. Hadn't she been warning herself not to think of her affair with Robbie as anything other than a brief interlude? But hearing Susan say the same thing made her want to protest. No, it wasn't just a passing fancy. It wasn't just an obsession of the flesh. Not for her, and not for Robbie either.

"I'm your friend." Susan patted Cathy's hand. "I don't want to see you hurt." Cathy drew in a deep breath and fought back the fear that Susan's words were starting to trigger. "Honey, you can't be naive enough to think... you're in for a lot of heartache if you don't start looking at things more realistically. What would Marilyn say?"

Cathy stifled a heated reply. "I think she'd be happy for me."

"Honey, Robbie is a more eligible match for Marilyn, and you know it." Susan's brow was furrowed with concern.

"Susan, Marilyn is old enough to remember the pure agony I went through when Jed left us. If any of the children are bitter toward their father, it's Marilyn. Believe me, I *know* my daughter would be happy to know—"

"But, Cathy, there's no future. Robbie is just beginning."

"And so am I!"

The words reverberated in Cathy's head as she walked Susan to the door a few minutes later. She *was* just beginning. Her whole life seemed to have taken a new direction since she'd met Robbie. Cathy was disappointed that Susan didn't fully approve of her and Robbie, but her arguments had helped Cathy put everything in better perspective. She was more certain than ever that her feelings for him were good and true.

- 9 -

ALONG WITH TORRENTIAL spring rains, the following two weeks brought Cathy a deluge of activities that consumed her every waking hour.

Amy returned. Although her presence meant that Cathy and Robbie couldn't be as free and uninhibited as they had been during spring vacation, Cathy was thrilled to see their relationship growing in new directions.

Her feelings for Robbie deepened. She continued to be amazed by the thudding of her heart the moment he came into view. She waited for the flush of their initial desire to subside, but it never did. Susan reminded her with increasing regularity that she would "see the light," but as April turned to May the only light that mattered was the light Cathy saw in Robbie's eyes whenever he looked at her.

"Mommy?"

Cathy looked up from the stack of blue books she had been grading all afternoon.

"The sun's out." Amy shifted back and forth on her skinny nine-year-old legs and gestured to Cathy's bedroom window, which overlooked a flowering cherry tree.

"You need new tennis shorts." Cathy smiled. Her daughter's long legs seemed to grow daily.

"Robbie was hoping you'd come to the courts with us." Amy's green eyes glowed with excitement. Before the torrential rains had struck, Robbie had started giving her tennis lessons. Ever since, Amy had been desperate for the sun to come out.

"I thought Robbie was planning to stay at the library until nine tonight." Cathy pulled Amy against her.

"He said he'd take me as soon as the courts are dry." Amy grinned.

"Amy Thomas, you didn't barge into the library at the first sign of the sun, did you? Robbie's writing a very important paper for his economics course, remember? He told you all about it." Cathy scanned her daughter's face.

"I just happened to be walking home from school when the sun came out." Amy stared guiltily at her sneakers, but before Cathy could reproach her further, the familiar sound of Robbie's car drifted up from the open window.

"Don't be mad, Mom!" Amy pleaded as she pumped Cathy's hand. "Come with us! Robbie wouldn't have suggested it if he'd had to study. Really, all I did was go in and say hi and he just *happened* to notice that the sun was out and he said the courts were probably already dry, or almost!"

Cathy laughed as she patted Amy on the behind. Of course she wasn't angry. After two weeks of rain who wouldn't want to play hooky on the first sunny afternoon?

The back door slammed, and Amy took off at a gallop to greet Robbie.

Cathy stared at herself in the mirror, and her smiling face reflected back the wonder of the past month.

Robbie had found his way into Amy's heart as easily as he had into hers.

Cathy pulled on a white Orange College sweat shirt over her blouse, ran a comb through her hair, and raced downstairs with a yelp of enthusiasm that matched her daughter's.

Robbie gave her a guilty grin as she bounded into the kitchen, and Amy stifled a giggle at the sight of his hand dangling over the open cookie jar.

"Those were supposed to be a surprise," Cathy admonished. She picked up a dishtowel and swatted Robbie's bare legs.

"Then you shouldn't have put them in the cookie jar." He stuffed a cookie in his mouth, grabbed Cathy around the waist, and hugged her fiercely.

"But they're *cookies!*" Amy squealed with delight as Robbie danced her mother back to the open container. "Cookies belong in the cookie jar."

Robbie eyed the child with mock seriousness. "Not when there's a chocolate chip addict on the loose. I smelled these cookies even before I turned into the lane. As a matter of fact, I smelled them on your dress when you came into the library."

"You did not!" Amy giggled.

"I did so." Robbie slipped his arm around Cathy's waist, and they headed outside toward his car, Amy jumping along next to them. "Didn't you eat one of those cookies for lunch?" Robbie asked Amy when they were seated in the car.

"You didn't smell cookies on my dress." Amy tapped him lightly on the shoulder.

"I wouldn't be surprised if he did," Cathy said.

"I'll make an experiment," Amy concluded after pondering for a few moments. "We'll just test him and see how good he is at *really* smelling chocolate chips. I'll make it very scientific."

Robbie laughed as he turned into the parking area adjacent to the town tennis courts. "I can't get away with anything with you, Amy. You always want proof!" He turned to Cathy. "The kid's a regular Einstein."

Cathy turned to grin at Amy, who sat beaming in the back seat.

"I'm serious, too," Amy called over her shoulder to Robbie as she raced onto the court. "I'm going to make an experiment with controls and everything."

"I know you are!" Robbie shouted back as he unzipped his navy blue tennis jacket and tossed it to Cathy to hold. "Watch her backhand," he told her as he turned to trot out onto the court.

Cathy nodded, plunked a canvas cushion down on the damp ground, and watched as Robbie began hitting balls to Amy's backhand. He was right; she was good. What a pleasure it was to hear Amy's laughter and to see the strengthening bond she was forming with Robbie. At times his deep and genuine delight with Amy's accomplishments astounded her. That was something Susan didn't see.

Cathy frowned, thinking of Susan's growing criticism. She was so certain that Cathy was perpetuating a dream that would inevitably end when Robbie graduated in June. Cathy turned her face up to the late afternoon sun. At times like this her sense of well-being outweighed her doubts and fears. She sniffed

the sweet, rain-freshened air and smiled dreamily as
Robbie and Amy continued to rally.

The next day was Saturday, and Cathy indulged in
an extra three hours of sleep. At the ungodly hour of
seven thirty Robbie had stopped by to pick up Amy
for an early tennis lesson before driving her to the
drop-off point for a Saturday night Brownie campout.
Bless Robbie. He had understood perfectly that they
would have to behave with greater propriety after
Amy's return. Their amorous meetings were confined
to Saturday nights, when Amy visited one of her
friends, or afternoons in Robbie's makeshift apartment.

"Sleepyhead!" Robbie popped his head into her
bedroom.

"You're not supposed to be here." Cathy's eyes
flew open with excitement. "You're supposed to be
in the library this morning. You can't play hooky two
days in a row."

"Who says?" Robbie sat down on the bed and leaned
over to kiss her. "You always smell so good when
you wake up, as if your body turns into spring flowers
when you sleep."

"Scented sheets." Cathy sat up and ran her hands
through his thick, blond hair.

"Amy's off," Robbie announced. "Along with
twenty giggling Brownies. Why don't we do that?"

"What?" Cathy ran her hand along his hard chest.

"Take the Brownies on a camping trip. I'd really
like to do that." He met her eyes mischievously.

"Just because the Brownies think you're so cute.

I've listened to Amy on the phone with her friends. If you don't watch out, the Brownies will make you run for office."

"I could be the first Brownie president!" Robbie chuckled, then turned serious. "I ran into Susan."

Cathy felt a flicker of nervousness.

"You know, Cath, she's worried about you. She didn't say she was, but I could tell by her manner. I think she thinks I'm some sort of playboy, some young gigolo who's trifling with her best friend." Robbie leaned over and untied his shoes.

Cathy shook her head. She didn't want to get into this, not on a bright, sparkling Saturday morning.

"She mentioned that someone has made another offer on the farm. Why didn't you tell me?" He turned to her.

Cathy shrugged. "I've put it out of my mind."

Robbie regarded her for a moment before continuing. "I found myself wanting to prove myself to Susan. We had coffee."

"You and Susan?" Cathy widened her eyes in surprise.

He nodded. "I told her the reason I'm going to Orange College is because I want to get to know this part of the country. Then when I take over my father's factories here I'll have some idea of how the people think. And then I invited her to dinner."

"You what!"

"I invited her and Ted to dinner tonight. Oh I'll cook, but . . ."

"Why?" Cathy felt her stomach churning nervously. "We agreed to keep things quiet until after graduation!"

"Cathy, come on. Do you really think Ted is going to bad-mouth you? I just think if Susan and Ted saw us together, then maybe..." Robbie broke off and eyed her closely. Cathy gnawed pensively at her lower lip. "I've noticed that there's always a strain between us after you talk with Susan," he went on. "I bet Susan says things that make you feel uncertain about *us*. Isn't that right?" Robbie peered closely at her.

Cathy sighed. "Yes... you're right."

A breeze shook the bough of the blossoming cherry tree outside her bedroom window. At least he was partly right, she admitted privately. Susan did say things that shook her confidence, but only because deep down she suspected they might be true. To a large degree she had succeeded in living in the present without trying to out-guess the future. Only on occasion did the prospect of Robbie's graduation send a shiver of fear through her. She simply could not visualize what would happen after June 7. Would he leave and that would be that? Would he leave and write letters, maybe make a visit, before time and distance wrote the final ending?

"You'd tell me if you needed to sell the farm, wouldn't you?" Robbie asked her.

Cathy looked away. "I probably wouldn't."

"But you should!" He sprang to his feet with an alarmed look.

"No." Cathy shook her head decisively. "No, I shouldn't. The farm's not your responsibility. It's mine."

"But you're not close to selling?"

"No." Cathy watched him carefully.

Obviously the farm meant a great deal to him. She had surmised before that it was all tied up in his mind with the happy family life he'd been denied while growing up.

Was it also somehow involved with his wanting a family . . . children . . . of his own? The question of children hadn't arisen since the night of Susan's party. Cathy knew he still didn't feel comfortable with her decision not to have more, no matter what commitment they made to each other. Surely he must have considered giving her up for a woman closer to his own age who was just starting out, like he was. But he was sensitive enough to her fears of losing him not to bring up the matter. An uneasy silence remained between them on the subject.

"I love you," he said, as if he had read her disquieting thoughts.

Cathy smiled and drew him down onto the bed. "I'm glad you asked Susan and Ted. Normal people have other couples to dinner, so tonight we'll be normal."

"I wish I could stay here all day." Robbie ran his hand lightly over the thin material of her nightgown.

"I have a ton of papers to grade," Cathy murmured as she arched her body toward him.

"And I have to drive over to Liberty for a meeting with one of our foremen. I've decided to interview ten workers and their families for a term paper on labor-management relations." He nuzzled her neck. "I'm going to use the paper as part of my argument with Dad. I know we can raise production in the Liberty and Valley Springs plants if we institute more worker incentives. I know it."

Cathy slipped her hands under his white tennis shirt and moved them in a circular motion over his chest.

"Why did you take your shoes and socks off if you're in such a hurry?" she whispered.

Robbie gave her a dazed smile. "I'm in a hurry but not in that much of a hurry. I'll just pop into your shower if you don't mind."

"I don't mind." Cathy kissed him tenderly and snuggled back under the covers as he stripped out of his clothes and headed for the bathroom.

"Leave the water on for me."

"I'll pick up chicken breasts, artichoke hearts, and some greens for dinner," he called above the noise of the shower. "Will you have time to make a dessert? I can do it, but . . ."

Cathy jumped out of bed and ran into the steamy bathroom. She stuck her head inside the glass shower stall. "It's okay. I'll have plenty of time to fix something for dessert. What time are they coming?"

"I told Susan you'd call her." Robbie leered at her and, without warning, whisked her under the shower.

"My nightgown!" Cathy cried.

"Umm!" Robbie picked up a tube of minty bath gel and began squirting it all over her.

"You nut!" Cathy shrieked as he began massaging the gel into her gown. When she was a mass of foam he stood back, water coursing off his broad back, and grinned. "I'm through." He stepped out of the shower, leaving her shaking with laughter.

"You owe me a new nightgown," Cathy yelled as she wriggled out of the foamy garment.

"The sky's the limit with you, sweetheart," he said in a thick Brooklyn accent and rapped on the shower stall door.

She emerged a few minutes later and toweled herself dry with a large salmon-colored towel that Robbie had given to her because he insisted it was the shade of her nipples when she was aroused.

As she reached for a bottle of orange and honey skin moisturizer, she sensed him standing in the bathroom doorway. She poured some of the rich emollient into her palm and began smoothing it on her shoulders. She could feel his eyes following every move. She looked up with a slight smile, meeting his eyes in the bathroom mirror. Her breath quickened as his expert fingers began to probe along the firm muscles of her lower back. As he spread a thin layer of cream over her back, Cathy gave in to the hypnotic sensation of his obliging touch.

"This is the way to start the day," he breathed as he sucked gently at the nape of her neck.

Cathy closed her eyes to enjoy more fully the voluptuous sensations that rushed through her body. His mouth, so warm and wet, made a slow path to one shoulder. She inhaled deeply as she felt his teeth prick against her tender skin, and her heart galloped furiously as he pressed his warm, naked body against her.

"My love," he whispered as he covered her breasts with his hands. Only then did he turn her slowly around to face him.

His eyes became heavy with desire as he gazed at Cathy's breasts, so erect and blushing from his touch. "Allow me." With painstaking control he began to lubricate her sensitive skin. His breathing grew ragged as his hands slipped along her torso, then circled around her bare stomach and back up to her full breasts.

Cathy caught her breath as she realized that his

intention was to surpass even their most torrid moments together.

He covered one breast with his long, tapering fingers while the other hand moved around her body and began to oil her back. When he pressed his naked body against hers, she gasped again and again as she tried to match his control, a control which would lead them inevitably to unknown heights of pleasure.

Now he moved away from her, and through half-closed lids she saw him kneel in front of her and begin to massage the lotion into her legs until she was as slippery as a sea creature. He clasped her ankles with his greasy hands and very deliberately moved up her legs to her sensitive inner thighs until she moaned with ecstasy. Then with an intensity that shook Cathy to her very core he began to move his mouth along the slippery trail created by his hands. She felt his fervent lips on her knees, her hips, the inside of her wrists, and finally, as he rose to his feet, he brought his mouth down hard on her own damp, longing lips.

She was nearly fainting with desire when he guided her back into the bedroom and lowered her gently to the bed. A soft fragrant breeze caressed her naked body, and she shivered slightly.

"I love this room." Robbie showered light kisses over her forehead. "A second-story window with a flowering cherry outside—what could be more perfect?"

"Even in winter," Cathy breathed, "even then it's perfect, with stark branches at the window."

"I can't wait." Robbie pressed his warm mouth against hers and covered her with his lean, powerful body. He slid his hands behind her and arched her gently into him.

Cathy closed her eyes, luxuriating in the hot force of his straining young body. Her mind felt clear, free of doubt. He would be there in winter. He would see the austere black branches of the cherry tree. He would be there!

"I love you!" Cathy opened her lips against his moist, demanding mouth. She kissed him with sudden urgency, as if her tongue, which made fiery forays into his mouth, could ensure their future together. She wanted everything from him. She wanted to give him everything. Deep in her heart she acknowledged the full extent of her desire for him. She wanted to live with him, marry him, share her life with him. At this heady moment, it seemed that her desire was born out of something as exquisitely simple and natural as the May breeze that wafted through her room.

With the entire force of her spirit she drove deeper and deeper into his mouth, challenging him and spurring him on until his control exploded in a shattering moan. He gripped her slippery body more tightly and rushed forward to that final, sublime moment that finally released them both from their delicious torment.

Cathy curled her head against his shoulder and breathed in the fragrance that was so uniquely his.

"Maybe after graduation we'll take a trip together." He kissed her damp hair lightly. It was the first mention he had made of future plans, and as simple as it was, she felt a thrill of excited expectation.

"A camping trip to Maine." He smoothed her hair. "Have you ever been there?"

Cathy shook her head. "Only in my dreams."

"And Paris?" he asked.

She smiled languidly up at him. "You can show me the world. The farthest west I've been is Chicago, the farthest east is New York City, for three days."

"Neophyte!" Robbie tweaked her cheek gently, and Cathy let out a little squeal. She sat up suddenly and smiled happily at him. She was actually looking forward to having dinner with Ted and Susan. For the first time she wasn't afraid. For the first time she longed to tell the world of her love for Robbie Darrow.

Twice she'd started a letter to Marilyn. Today she would finish it. For the first time, graduation didn't loom ahead of her as something to be feared.

"What is it?" Robbie seemed to sense her optimism.

"Just happy." Cathy swung her legs off of the bed. "I'm happy!" She threw her arms over her head and did a playful little jump.

Robbie leaped out of bed and took her hands in his. "Then that makes two."

By five o'clock that afternoon Cathy had graded all of her papers, vacuumed the house, painted the two closets in the guest house, and baked a sumptuous orange marmalade pie for dessert. After a gratifying phone conversation with her sons, she retired to the porch swing to wait for Robbie to come home. Susan and Ted weren't due to arrive until eight, and Robbie's chicken dish, one of his specialities, didn't take long to prepare.

When she heard his car turn into the lane, she jumped up and ran out to greet him. She was surprised that he had already changed for the evening, but the grim expression on his face made her stop short.

"What is it?"

"Problems." He shook his head. She had never seen him look so dejected.

"At the factory? What happened?" She led him back to the porch and pulled him into a seat. He was tense with suppressed anger, which surprised her, because he was usually so good at expressing it in a controlled way. Something had obviously upset him deeply.

"I had a big blowup with my dad." He didn't look at Cathy.

"What about? I didn't know your father was out here."

"I didn't either." Robbie's eyes were cold. Suddenly he seemed years older. "He fired several people . . . over my head. Technically he still owns everything, but it's supposed to be my turf. Anyway, he took matters into his own hands, which is what he usually does, and fifteen men who worked for Darrow Enterprises for the past ten to twenty years are now unemployed."

Cathy's stomach twisted in sympathy for him. She knew how devoted he was to the employees in his father's factories, knew that all of his future plans for the business were tied intimately to the workers. For some time now he had been trying to convince his father to set up a worker's cooperative whereby any worker who devised a technical improvement in production would be rewarded. The workers needed incentives, not just to do the job but to do *more* than the job. Robbie was willing to pay them for their efforts. His father wasn't even willing to try such a program.

"I'm sorry." Cathy wanted to reach out and hug him, but he seemed so aloof, so wrapped up in his own despair, that she held back. "Shall I call Susan and Ted?" she asked after several moments.

There was a distant look in his eyes when he finally glanced at her. He shook his head. "No, just give them my apologies. Cathy, I have to catch the next flight to New York."

"I see." She drew in a deep breath, needing desperately to be reassured that he was flying East on business and not at all because he was thinking of leaving her. "How long will you be gone?"

"Not long, I hope."

Cathy closed her eyes for a moment, trying to place her disappointment in the proper perspective. "We'll have dinner with Susan and Ted some other time," she offered with less conviction than she would have liked.

"Maybe I should call them myself."

"I'll take care of it." Cathy clasped his hand firmly.

"Damn!" he exploded after several moments of silence. "Fifteen men out of work for no good reason!"

He stood up and paced restlessly around the porch.

"I wish I could help." Cathy watched him helplessly. "If you and your dad could just talk . . . the way we talk. The way you've taught me to talk and listen."

Robbie shoved his hands deep into his pants pockets and walked over to the edge of the porch. He stared down at the pansies they had planted, his face drawn into a heavy scowl.

"Is that why you're going back East? So you can

talk it out with him?" she asked.

He shook his head. "Talking doesn't help where he's concerned."

"That's not like you," Cathy persisted. "You told me once that language, in every instance, is the most powerful tool we have."

Robbie shook his head adamantly. "Not with Raymond Darrow. Action is what counts with him. Words are gimmicks he uses like a magician."

"You make him sound so—"

"You don't know him!" Robbie turned on her suddenly, his anger spilling over.

Cathy stiffened and cautioned herself to tread lightly. Whatever had happened between Robbie and his father had wounded him deeply.

"He thinks I'm frittering away my time out here," Robbie went on. "He sees those interviews I went over to do today as a total waste of time. He can't stand it that I'm here in small-town Orange instead of mingling with the 'right' crowd at Harvard or Princeton."

"I didn't realize he was so against your finishing college here," Cathy observed.

"Oh, yes." Robbie paced back and forth. "He thinks I'm wasting time out here."

"You've made good marks. He should be pleased with that," Cathy ventured.

"You don't understand." Robbie turned on her again. "My father is not your typical papa who smiles and pats you on the head when you bring home a report card full of A's. The A's have to be from the right place. Your friends have to be the *right* people."

"Maybe you just don't understand what he's getting at," Cathy began tentatively. "Or maybe he can't see your particular individualism as anything other than a child's protest against parental authority. Maybe—"

"Stop defending him!" Robbie interrupted fiercely.

"I'm not!" she cried.

"You don't even know him, yet you're implying that he might have a point. He had no point in firing those men, or in a few of the other tactics he's been employing lately!" Robbie jerked his left hand out of his pocket and looked at his watch. "I was going to ask you to drive me to the airport, but maybe you don't want to."

"Of course I do!" Cathy sprang to her feet. How had they come so close to quarreling?

As she went inside to call Susan and get her purse, she warned herself against allowing Robbie's anger to color her feelings about his leaving. But it was almost as if he wanted to be angry at her too, as if she were somehow connected to the altercation between him and his father.

As she was about to dial Susan's number, she heard the back door slam shut and felt his hands on her shoulders. She replaced the receiver and turned to him.

"I love you." His eyes were luminous. "Please remember how deeply I love you."

She nodded and tried to keep her growing fear of losing him from showing in her eyes. Why was he saying all this if he was only going away for a few days?

She bit back the question. He needed her support now, not her fears. She stood on her tiptoes and ran a soothing hand through his hair. "I'll put the marmalade pie in the freezer." She smiled, though her eyes were damp. "We'll eat it when you get back."

- *10* -

THE FIRST FEW days after Robbie's departure were something of a revelation for Cathy. She felt relaxed and confident about both herself and her future with him. They had both grown over the past weeks and their love had deepened into something that felt very solid to her, even in his absence.

He had insisted that she drive his car while he was away and had laughed at her reservations, saying it would be foolish to turn down his offer in favor of tooling around in her sputtering Dart. He certainly had a point, and she adored him for suggesting it. She would have loved to drive it around, but it was too risky—especially after her indiscreet behavior at Susan's party. So she kept the car in her driveway, and just seeing it there was reassuring.

He phoned nightly, and Cathy would lie in bed listening to his low, seductive voice promising that as soon as they were together he would make up for the hours of separation. He was still vague when talking about what he was doing in New York, but she knew it concerned the business and the argument he'd had with his father. It was odd that he didn't tell her more about what was going on, since he usually bounced all of his professional ideas around with her. But she decided not to pressure him, knowing that the problem with his father was a double-edged sword, emotional as well as professional.

But by Wednesday a gnawing ache was growing in her. She asked herself what business was so important that it would take him away for so long less than a month before graduation.

Amy's constant inquiries didn't help either. Her daughter seemed almost as desperate for Robbie's return as she was. Whenever the telephone rang, the little girl ran to answer it and was disappointed when it wasn't Robbie.

Although Susan had accepted the canceled dinner engagement with her usual good grace, Cathy knew that the last-minute change had netted Robbie another strike against him. She could practically hear Susan's mind clicking off the words *young and unreliable*.

Still, it was important to Cathy that such a long-term friendship not disintegrate, so when Susan phoned and asked Cathy to lunch at the country club after her Thursday class, Cathy agreed. Susan declared it was business, from which Cathy surmised it had to do with yet another offer on the farm. She intended to put a stop to the ridiculous offers once and for all.

When Cathy joined Susan at the table, the first words out of Susan's mouth were, "I must say you look terrific."

Cathy grinned and touched a hand to her hair, which was pulled back from her face and fastened with two barrettes. Her hairdo made her feel attractive. Thinking about Robbie made her feel happy and calm. "I feel good," she said. "Except I miss Robbie. Susan, I'm the one to blame for the misconceptions you have about him. I've been hiding him."

Susan shook her head skeptically. "Says who? And I don't blame you for being discreet."

"But I don't need to be, with you and Ted. Robbie pointed that out to me." Cathy leaned forward intently. It was important to her that Susan understand.

"I had a nice cup of coffee with him," Susan said. "He's nice. I have nothing against him personally." She paused. "I guess you think I'm pretty narrow-minded for disapproving of you two."

Cathy shook her head. "No, I know you have my best interests at heart."

"I do," Susan affirmed. "If you said to me, 'I'm having a wild fling, we spend all day in bed, and I can't think of a thing to say to him,' I'd be thrilled. But what I hear and sense from you is ... it's like adolescent love. Now don't get mad."

"I'm not mad." Cathy sipped her coffee pensively. "But I'm not having just a wild fling. I enjoy talking to him. He's a fascinating man, Susan. He lived in London for a year, he spent one summer working on a cargo ship, he's been involved in his father's business since he was eighteen. He has definite ideas of his own. He's ... I feel like I'm trying to sell him to you, but it's only because I care about you both. If only we all could have had dinner the other night, you'd have seen for yourself."

"Cath," Susan interjected, "you're so smitten you've lost touch with reality."

"No I haven't." Cathy stared briefly into the distance. In a way she wished she *had* lost touch with reality. Then maybe the ultimate problem of children wouldn't continue to haunt her.

"Can I tell you what I think?" Susan asked somberly.

"Wouldn't you anyway?" Cathy smiled.

Susan nodded and rushed on. "I don't want to see you pick up and leave Orange, Cathy. God knows what I'd do without you around, but I think the reason you've flipped over someone like Robbie is that things are too dull here. You know, everything in a small town like this is couples, and I can see that from your point of view there's very little opportunity to meet an interesting man. You need a more adventurous environment, like Columbus or Cincinnati. If you don't want to sell the farm, you could even commute. But at least you'd be out in the mainstream, with an opportunity to meet men your own age and—"

"Susan, there's one thing wrong with your reasoning," Cathy interrupted calmly, "though I appreciate the thought you've given this. I wasn't unhappy when I first met Robbie. On the contrary, I felt fabulous the first day I laid eyes on him. I even felt skinny and firm and young! *Before* I met him. He didn't make me feel those things. I think my ability to get involved with him is a sign of my growth, not a sign of neurosis or malcontentedness."

Susan shook her head dubiously. They were at a standstill. "What will he do after graduation?" she asked after a moment.

"He'll be involved in some capacity with his father's business."

"Where does that leave you?"

Cathy felt a wave of doubt pass over her, but she smiled. "His father owns several companies in the area. That's why Robbie decided to finish school at Orange."

Susan sighed deeply and accepted her defeat with

a gracious smile. "Well, I guess you know what you're doing. Now——" Susan rubbed her chubby hands together in preparation for the next order of business which, as Cathy had guessed, had to do with yet another offer from some still nameless party to buy the farm.

"Why can't you tell me who it is?" Cathy asked.

"I don't even know, but it's not unusual for someone, either a private party or a company, to make an offer on a property in someone else's name. Keeps the price from going up."

Cathy laughed. "They're the ones who are raising the price. I haven't said a word."

"You know what I mean. If somebody really rich wants to buy something, a lot of sellers would raise the price." Susan popped a stick of gum into her mouth and offered one to Cathy.

Cathy shook her head. "Okay, I'll meet their representative, but don't get excited about making a sale, Sus. I'm only doing it out of curiosity."

Susan flushed. "You don't think I'd——"

"No." Cathy waved her off. "I know you have my best interests at heart . . . in *all* matters."

"Mommy! The phone!" Amy raced out the back door when Cathy pulled up in the driveway. From her excited tone Cathy knew the call was from Robbie.

Thank God! She grabbed the two bags of groceries and ran inside. She was pleased with herself for not succumbing to Susan's concern about Robbie, but the old doubts were beginning to return. The longer he stayed away, the harder it was going to be not to start protecting herself. She needed those long-distance phone calls and now, especially now, she was desperate to hear his voice.

"Mr. Darrow, Mr. Darrow. It's Mr. Darrow." Amy jumped up and down alongside her mother as Cathy set the groceries on the kitchen table and hurried into the living room.

"Oh it is, is it?" Cathy batted her eyes at Amy. "Hello, Mr. Darrow," she breathed into the receiver in a low, sultry voice that made Amy giggle and jump with excitement.

"Is this Mrs. Thomas?" Cathy froze at the unfamiliar voice on the other end of the wire. She frowned at Amy and waved at her to stop jumping up and down. It wasn't like Amy to joke around.

"Yes," she said cautiously.

"This is Mr. Darrow, Robbie's father." The voice was as stern and humorless as Robbie's voice was beguiling.

"Oh, I'm sorry." Cathy caught her breath. "I really thought . . ."

"I think I know what you thought," said the voice. "This is Raymond Darrow."

"Yes." Cathy nodded tensely. "Is Robbie all right?"

"Of course he's all right. In the way you mean, in any case." There was a brief pause. "Mrs. Thomas, I'd like to meet you for dinner."

Cathy met her daughter's frightened blue eyes and smiled, signaling that there was nothing to worry about. "I'd love to. When?"

"Tonight," Raymond Darrow answered curtly.

It was nearly six o'clock and he expected her to meet him tonight? "Mr. Darrow, I have a daughter."

"Yes, I know."

"I would have to find a baby-sitter. Could we make it some other night? Tomorrow?" Cathy clutched the receiver nervously.

"Tomorrow's impossible. It's very important, Mrs. Thomas."

Of course it was, she thought. Everything that Raymond Darrow did was very important, at least to Raymond Darrow. When Robbie had described his father's coldness, Cathy had assumed that at least a degree of his harshness stemmed from Robbie's own lack of objectivity. She knew how difficult it was for parents and children to judge each other fairly. But after speaking with Raymond Darrow for only a few minutes, she agreed completely with Robbie's assessment. She would have liked to decline; certainly she had a valid excuse in Amy. But there was too much at stake. He was, after all, Robbie's father.

"I'll find a way, Mr. Darrow." Cathy made an effort to sound friendly. "I'll need at least an hour and a half to get myself squared away."

"I'm at the Holiday Inn off of Interstate Seventy-one. I'll make the reservation for eight. Will that give you enough time?"

"Oh yes." Cathy's sense of humor returned, and she imagined herself adding, "How gracious of you to give me an extra half an hour."

Amy's eyes were large with curiosity as Cathy hung up. "Who was it?"

"Mr. Darrow is Robbie's father." Cathy patted Amy's head and returned to the kitchen to scramble up some sort of dinner for the child.

"I didn't think it sounded like Robbie's voice."

Amy helped Cathy put the groceries away. "But I thought it was one of his jokes. You know, calling himself Mr. Darrow in that funny voice."

"Ah yes." Cathy stood on tiptoe to put a five-pound bag of sugar in the top cupboard. "Well, this should be interesting, Amy. I'll give Susan a call and see if it's okay for you to go over there while I'm at dinner. Is that all right, honey? You can do your homework there, and I'll pick you up on my way home. I'm sure I won't be late. I can't imagine what I'll say to Mr. Raymond Darrow."

Cathy agonized over what to wear to dinner with Raymond Darrow. Finally she settled on one of her favorite outfits, a hunter-green linen dress that accented her eyes and set off her pale, creamy complexion. To compensate for shuttling Amy around so at the last minute, she fixed her a deluxe cheeseburger and indulged her in a chocolate shake made in the blender. Finally she and Amy climbed into the Dart and drove off.

Cathy entered the dimly lit dining room at the Holiday Inn half an hour later and recognized Raymond Darrow instantly.

He stood up as she approached and held out her chair. "Mrs. Thomas."

Cathy cautioned herself to maintain her sense of humor, for that, she was certain, was the only way she would survive Raymond Darrow and the inquisition he no doubt had in store for her.

Like his son, he was dashingly handsome, tall and lean and, Cathy guessed, probably in his early fifties. His blond hair, though not as curly as Robbie's, was the same thick, coarse mop, and the only gray in evidence was at the temples. Cathy found it almost eerie to sit across from an older version of Robbie. The resemblance was uncanny.

But the similarity went only skin deep. By the time the waiter had delivered their dinners, Cathy wondered how she had thought even for a moment that Raymond Darrow looked like his son. He possessed none of Robbie's gentleness, none of his humor or eagerness. Whereas Robbie's blue eyes laughed or reflected the depth of his true feelings, Raymond's blue eyes were expressionless. He looked at his menu with the same aloofness with which he viewed Cathy, and he smiled only once, a perfunctory grimace to the waiter, who made the mistake of bringing him an olive with his martini instead of a twist of lemon.

He was so formidable to Cathy that he seemed unreal to her and thus presented less of a problem. To her surprise she found herself relaxing. Surely she had nothing to lose since he had obviously already made up his mind about her.

He waited until they had finished their entrees, then came straight to the point. "Mrs. Thomas, I'm quite used to extricating my son from difficult circumstances. I think you should know that this is not the first time Robert has blundered into a romantic adventure that everyone, other than himself, perceives as being quite out of the question."

Cathy nodded and saw a slight astonishment color his expression as he noted her composure.

"Mr. Darrow," she began softly, "Robbie was very upset when he returned from Liberty on Saturday. I know the two of you have a long-running debate about how precisely to run your business, and I don't want to get into that. But I think you should know that Robbie has poured his heart and soul into his scheme for the Liberty and Valley Springs factories. He's not doing it to . . . to *get* you. He would like your respect, if not your blessing, for his ideas."

"So you know of all these plans?" Mr. Darrow studied her with steely eyes.

"You must know your son likes to talk." Cathy's face broke into a warm smile. "If there's anyone to listen, he'll talk. I happen to like that about him."

Mr. Darrow nodded tightly. "Twenty-five is rather late to be graduating from college."

"I suppose," Cathy admitted. "I'm sure Robbie's given you plenty of cause for concern. But maybe he's finally found himself, so to speak. And maybe you just haven't noticed the change in him. Sometimes we get stuck in our reactions to people, especially our children. My oldest daughter is a woman, for example, but I have to constantly remind myself that I'm no longer the sole provider of Band-Aids and sympathy. You don't know me, and my opinion may not mean much, but I've rarely known anyone as dedicated and serious about his work as Robbie is."

"My son doesn't know I've . . . arranged this dinner." Raymond Darrow reached for his wineglass, then stopped, his hand in midair. "You're not what I expected, Mrs. Thomas."

"Please call me Cathy." She met his eyes directly, and for the first time she detected a glimmer of acceptance in them.

Mr. Darrow frowned. "Last Saturday, Robert told me that he'd taken up with a woman with four children. It seemed wrong, like another of his rebellious gestures. I have two other sons. Neither of them is at all like Robert. Between you and me, they don't interest me as much as my youngest son does, although it's always been difficult for Robert and me to get along."

Cathy smiled sympathetically. "Robbie felt terrible on Saturday."

Mr. Darrow sighed. "I don't approve of all of his notions. In a year his scheme for worker creativity would prove financially disastrous."

Cathy nodded. "I know what you're saying, but I don't think that's what's really important here. I can't argue the merits of one economic system over another, but there should be some way of testing Robbie's plan to see if it works. Unless your business is teetering on the brink of bankruptcy, there should be a way to implement his plan on a small scale, just to see."

Raymond Darrow cast Cathy a vaguely amused smile. "You're very convincing."

"That's only because I'm not your son." Cathy laughed.

"I didn't come here to compliment you." He looked at her steadily. "I see I shall end by doing so. I like you."

"Thank you." Cathy accepted the compliment graciously, but she was acutely aware of the tension between them.

A short time later Mr. Darrow walked Cathy outside to the parking lot. "Perhaps you and Robbie and I can have dinner together before I fly back East. You might mention it to him."

"Yes, yes, I will," she said automatically, but she

was astonished to realize that Mr. Darrow didn't know Robbie had flown back East. If Robbie's business matters didn't have anything to do with his father, and apparently they didn't, what *was* he doing?

Somehow Cathy managed to remain calm while she picked up Amy at Susan's, then took her home and saw her to bed. But once alone her imagination, held so tightly in check over the past few weeks, ran rampant with possible scenarios. He had gone back East because of someone. Someone he was going to break off with? Someone he still loved or thought he loved? Cathy stared at the phone, willing it to ring. Perhaps he had called while she was out with his father.

She crawled into bed knowing full well she wouldn't be able to sleep. Suddenly she was angry at Robbie for not letting her know how she could reach him. Tonight, when she needed to hear his voice, it felt wrong not to be able to contact him.

"Damn!" Cathy threw back the covers and jumped out of bed. She paced around the room several times and finally went downstairs to sit at the kitchen table and drink a cold beer. Susan swore that drinking beer before bed would subdue any tormenting problem.

What was she going to do? It suddenly seemed to Cathy that unless she answered that question she would never sleep. What was she going to do about Robbie Darrow, and what was she going to do about her entire life? Maybe Susan was right. Maybe it was time to move on . . .

With her reduced work load at the college she was just barely squeaking by financially. If there was another cutback next fall, which was quite possible, what would she do then? One thing was becoming more clear. She couldn't ignore the offer to buy the farm. Tomorrow, when she met the prospective buyer's representative, a Ms. Farrell, she would have to approach the meeting with more than curiosity.

Sell the farm? She chewed her lip, then got out a pad and pencil and did some figuring. If there was another job cutback, she wouldn't have a choice. She'd have to sell the farm.

Maybe she should move away. Amy was still young enough to adapt to a new school and friends. If she was going to make a move, this would be the best time to do it. But wouldn't she be doing just what Robbie had been afraid she'd do, closing him off? Well, it was his own fault for staying away so long, for not calling.

Suddenly she knew the answer to at least one of the questions plaguing her. She did not want to have another family. As much as she loved Amy, she had to admit she'd be glad when the last baby was fully grown and reasonably independent. She'd been tied down and diligent all of her life. Now she wanted her freedom.

Back upstairs, the bed was just as empty and her nerves just as jangled as before. So much for the cold-beer remedy, she thought, rolling over onto one side and pounding her pillow to get comfortable. She lay perfectly still, waiting for the sense of relief that usually followed a major decision.

She was still waiting when the phone rang.

"It's me," Robbie said quietly. "I'm back."

In spite of all the doubts and questions that had raged through her since her meeting with Raymond

Darrow, Cathy felt overwhelmed with relief. She stretched, catlike as if he were already there beside her.

"How did you get back? When? Where are you? Are you at the airport?" He laughed as she fired off the barrage of breathless questions.

"I flew. Tonight at eight. My apartment. No." Even teasing his voice was seductive, and Cathy felt an erotic tug in the pit of her stomach. "I tried phoning you from LaGuardia before the plane took off, then I tried again when we landed in Columbus at about seven forty-five. You wretch, you were out kicking up your heels. When can I come over and make up for lost time? I want to feel that little body... I've missed you!"

"I've missed you too!" Cathy said feelingly. "But I have an early class and..."

"Amy's asleep." He mimicked her words as she spoke them. "I want to make love to you." His words made her flush with longing. She paused, considering. "I'll be very quiet," he urged. "I'll call that derelict cab company and be out in ten minutes. Okay?"

She craved him in every way possible. The sound of his voice had almost obliterated her earlier thoughts.

"Darling," he said, "are you there or have you dozed off?"

Cathy laughed at the ridiculous notion. "I'll dazzle you," he promised huskily. "I've dreamed up all sorts of titillating projects for us to experiment on. Would you like to hear?"

"Robbie!" Cathy's pulse raced. She could almost feel his sensitive fingers easing their way toward their mark. "Now you've made it impossible for me to sleep," she told him in a throaty voice.

"That was my intention." He gave a devilish laugh.

She wondered what he would say when she told him she'd met his father. There was so much to tell him. She dropped back against the pillow, shaking her head. Was she losing her mind? Where were all of those doubts, all of those plans and new beginnings?

"And I have a surprise," he baited her further. As if she needed it...

"Robbie," she began, but he interrupted.

"You're going to say no. I can hear it in your voice." He sounded devastated.

"I am saying no. It's one o'clock. You have a class at ten. I have one at eight."

"I love you," he said without further protest. "I'll expect you at my pad for lunch, if you get my drift. Actually I did bring back lunch. Some special New York pastrami just for you, and all the pickles we can eat."

"I'll be there." Cathy smiled as he blew her a sexy kiss. She replaced the receiver and waited for her inner turmoil to return, but all she could think of was that he had come back with the same love and enthusiasm for her that he had left with. Somehow that thought outweighed everything else.

- *11* -

WHOEVER HAD HIRED Jeanne Farrell to represent their case in the purchasing of her farm had an incredibly good business sense, Cathy thought as she left the meeting and began walking toward Robbie's apartment. In the light of day the desire to sell had waned. Still, Ms. Farrell had been impressive, if only because she was so understanding and put absolutely no pressure on Cathy.

Ms. Farrell was Cathy's age, and although she dressed with a New York flair, she understood perfectly how Cathy would be loath to part with such a beautiful estate. In fact, the prospective buyer was willing to lease Cathy the house and a surrounding three acres. Whoever he/she was—and that was how Ms. Farrell phrased it—was only interested in the back acreage. She mentioned the latest figure of $750,000 without batting an eye. She was flying back to her office in New York, but Cathy could phone her any time for further information.

It began to drizzle just as Cathy turned down Robbie's street. By the time she pounded on his door, she was drenched. It didn't matter to him. He clasped her soaked body to him and lifted her off the floor, hugging her. Before she could utter so much as a hello, his warm, dry mouth was pressing against her lips. Her wet clothes forgotten, Cathy eagerly gave entrance to his probing tongue. How she'd missed him!

She swung her arms around his neck, drawing him deeper inside, and gasped at the heady demands of his thrusting movements. She felt his desire for her more acutely than ever before. Usually he was capable of pulling back, but today his need for her was wild, too hungry to control.

He pulled Cathy across the room until they reached the mattress that he had placed on the rug and used as a bed. He ran his tongue around her mouth as if even the raindrops were a part of her to be savored.

"Next time you come with me or I come back sooner." He began to unbutton her blouse with hot, feverish fingers. She reached down and lifted those long, tapering fingers she had come to love. She tasted them and felt a heightened sense of expectancy as he removed her soaked blouse uttering, "Tell me you missed me, Cathy. Tell me how much."

As his hands covered her firm breasts, she moaned her reply and fell against him. He circled one nipple with his tongue while his hands unfastened the hook on her cotton skirt and drew down the zipper. Cathy began to unfasten his buckle. She had been waiting for this for nearly five days...five days that had seemed an eternity.

She trembled with anticipation as he slithered out of his jeans and tossed them aside. For a moment he stood over her, naked, and she gazed up at him in wonder at the absolute beauty of his body. As muscular as he was, the impression was nevertheless one of smoothness, as in an exquisite piece of sculpture.

As he lowered himself to her, she ran her hand along his hard thigh until she reached his knee. Then she grasped him, urging him on as his hot, pulsating body joined with hers.

Cathy's passion was building with a force that left her gasping. Robbie raised himself over her on his elbows, moving harder and harder until she clutched him with all of her strength and shut her eyes in mindless ecstasy. As they burst like mutual flames into a sea of erotic oblivion, she loosened her grasp and her body went limp.

"That was just the beginning," Robbie panted. "The aperitif, so to speak . . . before the main course."

Cathy couldn't think to reply. She ran her hands through his hair, which was now as wet as her own. For a long while they lay without speaking, listening to the rhythm of the gentle, soothing rain on the pavement below. Curled on one side, Cathy nestled her head into Robbie's firm, young chest and felt her eyelids droop. For the moment, Ms. Farrell, the farm, her job—everything—seemed very remote.

When she awoke, it was still raining, and the day had grown even more dreary and dark. Robbie had tacked a note to his pillow saying he'd gone to class.

Cathy squinted groggily at her watch, which she had placed on the floor next to the mattress. Nearly three in the afternoon! She felt a sinking, wasted feeling in the pit of her stomach. She tried telling herself it was all right; she'd needed the rest. But she never napped in the afternoon, and the fact that an entire day was now practically gone made her feel anxious.

Suddenly she remembered that it was her day to pick up Amy and Maybeth from their dance class.

She struggled to her feet and turned on the one lamp next to the mattress. Robbie had thoughtfully hung her wet clothes on the shower rod in the bathroom, but they were still damp and she winced as she slipped into the clammy blouse.

As she gathered up her purse and satchel, she realized her legs were wobbling. She sank into one of Robbie's canvas director's chairs.

Yes, he had returned. Yes, he loved her and desired her. But... she looked around his spartanly furnished apartment, feeling confused and dazed. This was a student's apartment. He was content to live this basic, no-frills existence because he was so young, because he was still mostly a nomad, like Marilyn and her friends.

Why hadn't it occurred to her before that Robbie's carefree existence closely resembled Marilyn's? She even had a mattress on the floor of her apartment. And that was fine; those details were appropriate for young people who were just starting out. But how did Robbie reconcile her own cozy, antique-filled home with his simple, uncluttered lifestyle? She could see he liked to move freely between the two worlds, but wasn't that the point? Robbie was still growing. He was unsettled, as Susan had said. Oh, he loved teaching Amy to play tennis, but would he really be willing to take on all the responsibilities associated with being the father of a nine-year-old girl?

And how could she have been so blind and self-absorbed not to have considered Amy's feelings in the matter? Amy, who became more attached to him daily. Ever-hopeful little Amy, who had never had a father on a day-to-day basis. Cathy dug in her purse for a tissue. Her youngest daughter was very perceptive. It had probably not escaped her that her mother's relationship with this man was entirely different from the casual friendships Cathy usually formed. Amy was probably nourishing a dream of her own in which she was flanked by two smiling, loving parents—Robbie and Cathy.

"How could I have been so selfish?" Cathy bolted up from the director's chair. Time after time Jed had urged her to marry someone for Marilyn and Amy's sake. But no, she had been too stubborn or too afraid or too . . . something. She had been too selfish. She had wanted something more than a marriage of convenience. She had wanted love, and now where had it landed her?

It wasn't even simply a question of the children she wasn't willing to have. No, she had missed the implication of *Amy*'s involvement. She had been so overjoyed that Robbie and her daughter got along so well that it hadn't occurred to her how much Amy, too, would suffer when he left.

She tugged at her wrinkled skirt in an effort to look presentable. As she started for the door, her eye was drawn to a pile of packages, all, she noted, with wilted ribbons. She poked her finger tentatively inside a large shopping bag from Saks Fifth Avenue, noticing the two large boxes and several smaller ones. She picked up an oblong box and moved it through the air. She'd be willing to wager it was a tennis racket for Amy.

Suddenly she turned away in a flood of tears. It would be much easier if he weren't so damned thoughtful and generous. She had to talk to him. She'd been procrastinating long enough. She had to settle their relationship once and for all.

Just then Robbie's phone rang. She stared at it, half tempted to answer it. Who could it be? Maybe it was his father. She had altogether forgotten to mention their dinner together to Robbie.

She shook her head. Now that he had actually returned, she was grasping for everything negative she could find to use against him. Why? She caught her breath. Because she loved him too much. Because the panic of not having him in her life made her numb.

She told herself to be patient. He had only just returned. There would be time to talk. But there wasn't enough time, and she had Amy to consider.

The phone stopped ringing, but Cathy continued to stand in the middle of the nearly empty living room staring at it. Suddenly she remembered his car. That meant he'd have to come out to the farm, probably tonight.

She didn't feel up to talking to him tonight, and she certainly didn't want to do it at her house. She wanted someplace public, some neutral location that wasn't fraught with so many memories.

The phone rang once, then stopped. Cathy turned her back on it and started for the door. She paused as it rang three more times, stopped, rang once more, stopped, and rang three times. She knew it was Robbie. He would think of something like that, some signal that would give her permission to answer his phone.

She considered ignoring his signal, but immediately dismissed the idea. When the phone rang again, she answered it.

"Thank God you're there." He sounded rushed. "I wanted to take you and Amy out to dinner tonight, but my little junket back East has set me back. I have a lot of reading to get through before I can even think of starting to review for finals."

"Don't worry." Cathy felt as if someone had given her a stay of execution.

"I'm not worried about finals," he said, "I'm worried about not spending time with you. I want to! I want *you!*"

Cathy drew in a deep breath. She didn't want to clue him in to her emotional state. He was a top student, but even so, he would need to concentrate fully on studying for his finals.

"Listen," he went on briskly. "Isn't it time to pick up Amy from her dance class?"

How had he remembered Amy's dance lesson? Cathy's lip began to tremble. "I was just about to leave," she said faintly, and was relieved when he didn't pick up on the tears that spilled slowly from her eyes.

"Saturday!" he announced with his usual exuberance. "Saturday all day and all night, okay? Don't worry about the car," he added as if having read her mind. "I don't need it."

"Saturday it is." Cathy forced herself to speak calmly.

"Give Amy a kiss for me and . . . hey! Take along that box marked Arnold's. I wanted to see her face, but I'll wait until she opens one of my other goodies.

And you?" He chuckled maliciously. "Wait till you see what I have in store for you. You didn't peek, did you?"

"No, I didn't peek."

"I love you . . . and I'm signing off. Over and out." He blew her a kiss and the phone went dead.

After picking up Amy and Maybeth, Cathy drove back to the farm, changed into a pair of navy wool slacks and a white sweater to accommodate the chilly wet weather, and took the girls to the nearest fast food hamburger place. Splurging on milk shakes and fries and watching her daughter's enthusiasm for this rare treat took Cathy's mind off Robbie. She was drawn into the girlish chatter about dance class, the fourth-grade class picnic, and boys. Amy's laughter was like a balm to her, and she returned to the car with both arms thrown around the girl's slender shoulders.

After tucking Amy into bed that night, Cathy watched television, sewed on a few buttons, and pressed a dress to wear to work the next day. On impulse she phoned Marilyn and was gratified to learn that her oldest daughter's summer plans included returning home. She had gotten a job assisting one of the psychology professors in a clinical experiment. Cathy hung up smiling with anticipation at the thought of having Marilyn home for three months.

And what about Robbie? She frowned as she put the ironing board away. She wished tomorrow were Saturday so they could discuss everything that was bothering her. Until then she would simply try not to think about it.

- *12* -

SATURDAY DAWNED BRIGHT and sunny, with unseasonably high temperatures more appropriate to June than May. Cathy had risen early, showered, and dressed in clean jeans and a T-shirt. By eight she and Amy had finished a breakfast of French toast, and Amy was outside hoeing at a vague plot she called her garden.

Cathy puttered nervously around the house. Wanting to be alone with Robbie, she had arranged for Amy to spend the day with Maybeth. He would object, of course. His plan included Amy, but Cathy knew it was for the best not to involve the child further.

She expected Robbie to phone when he got up, then, when she drove in to pick him up, she would drop Amy off on the way. She had given no thought to what precisely she was going to say to him, but she was secure in the logistics of the day, which gave her at least some confidence.

When the phone rang at eight thirty, Cathy was surprised to find it was Susan wanting to know how her meeting with Ms. Farrell had gone.

"I'm really considering it," Cathy told her. "I may be coming to my senses."

"Oh, Cath..." Susan's voice was full of sympathy. "If you need me, if you need to talk, I'm here. Are you okay?"

"More or less," Cathy admitted. "Sus, I don't want to talk right now. Maybe I'll see you tonight. Will you and Ted be around?"

"I'll make it a point to be around, honey. Now you just call, okay?"

Cathy heaved a sigh as she hung up. She dreaded the day ahead.

"Hey, let's get a move on!" The back door slammed shut as Robbie bounded inside, dressed in his tennis whites. He grabbed Cathy around the waist and dipped her backward in a dramatic kiss.

"How did you . . ." she began, confused, but before she could finish Amy raced by and flew up the stairs, calling back that she was going to put on her tennis shoes.

So much for the security provided by all of those logistics, Cathy thought. She couldn't very well forbid them to play tennis now that Robbie was actually here, could she?

"Yum." Robbie smelled of a citrusy shaving lotion as he pressed his mouth on hers. His tongue teased her lips, and his hand covered her behind as he pressed her against him. Clearly he hadn't sensed any of the doubts that had dominated her thinking since his return.

He pulled away, grinning sheepishly as he glanced upstairs to where Amy had just disappeared.

"How did you get here?" Cathy didn't know whether to laugh or look stern.

"Jogged," he announced, kicking up his long, lean legs, which appeared almost tanned in contrast with his white shoes and socks. "Got anything for me to eat?"

Cathy shook her head as he followed her into the kitchen and began poking around in her refrigerator. She turned to see him running his finger around the rim of Amy's dirty breakfast plate. "Maple syrup?" He looked crestfallen. "You made pancakes without me?"

"French toast." Cathy felt all of her resolve melting.

He pouted in mock hurt, and she moved behind him and rested her cheek on his back.

He turned and pressed his lips lovingly against her hand. "I cracked a lot of books over the past few days. I think I'll ace all my finals."

"I wouldn't be surprised."

"Thanks for being so understanding." He looked steadily up at her. His eyes were clear and unconcerned. She felt guilty knowing that another few hours would go by with him still believing everything was fine between them.

"I brought back stuff for a picnic," he said, pulling her down on his lap. "We'll have a perfect day, just the three of us."

"Robbie," she began, "Amy has plans. She's spending the day with Maybeth."

"So we'll bring Maybeth along." He held her face in his hands and studied her intently. "What's the matter, Cath?"

"Nothing! Really nothing." Cathy hugged him and hopped off his lap. Why not have the day, she decided suddenly, one last day with the two children. She would tell him tonight, after Amy had gone to spend the night with Maybeth.

Just then Amy skipped into the kitchen, eager to

begin her tennis lesson. "You have a beautiful mother," Robbie told her.

"I know." Amy's eyes danced as she took Robbie's hand and led him out the kitchen door.

He waved over his shoulder. "We'll be back in an hour. We'll pick Maybeth up on our way."

They spent the afternoon following trails that wound through one of the old Indian sites some twenty miles from Orange. They trudged up steep hills and listened to Robbie explain about the famous Indian mound builders. Cathy had had no idea he was so knowledgeable about the subject, but this seemed just another unexpected facet to his personality. He made light of his knowledge. The mound builders, he insisted, were just another one of his many tangents.

They picnicked near a stream. After they were finished eating, they all took off their shoes and socks and went wading. Cathy found it impossible not to lose herself in the hilarity of the moment when Robbie—she guessed it was on purpose, to entertain the girls—fell into the swirling water.

Robbie came out of the water dripping and laughing. "Well, it sure is warm today, but not warm enough for these," he said, pointing to the wet clothes plastered to his body, then beginning to rummage through his tennis bag for dry clothes.

"It sure feels like summer to me," Amy teased.

"Oh yeah?" he said, starting to push her toward the water. When she squealed, he gave her an affectionate pat on the behind and disappeared into the bushes to change.

Cathy and the girls gathered their belongings, and

when Robbie joined them, they all trudged back to the car, tired from the day's activities.

Yes, thought Cathy as they drove toward town in silence, it certainly did feel like summer. But suddenly she felt a chill. Now the day was over, and she knew she couldn't allow things to continue without talking of the future. She didn't know what she would say, but somehow she would do it tonight.

Robbie ran back to the car after dropping Amy and Maybeth off at Maybeth's house. "And now the best part." His eyes were brimming with desire as he leaned over the stick shift and kissed Cathy with soft, warm lips.

"Robbie..." Cathy's lips parted instinctively. Now, they had to talk now.

"Yes?" He ran the tip of his tongue along her parted lips and made quick forays inside as she tried to focus on what she had to do. "What's on your mind, Cathy? You scare me when you look like that." He turned the key in the ignition and began to drive toward the farm.

Cathy agonized a moment, then said, "I guess a lot happened while you were away."

"You promised not to jump to any conclusions while I was gone. You promised to let time take care of..." He broke off and glared at the road ahead.

"Some promises can't be kept," she said slowly. Oh, how she wanted to say it just right, but her mind wouldn't work. She didn't know where to begin. "Robbie, I can't go on seeing you," she blurted out.

He glanced briefly at her, as if to see if she was serious.

"Why the hell not?" he exclaimed angrily, and the MG shot ahead.

"I think you should slow—"

"Well, I think *you* should slow down." He turned to glare at her. "What are you talking about . . . not seeing me? We just had a perfect day. What the hell do you want?"

Cathy felt her own temper flare. She had never seen him this angry before, and it unnerved her.

"It's not good for Amy," she began tightly.

"I can't believe what I'm hearing!" Robbie turned the corner too sharply and the tires squealed.

"I said slow down!" Cathy raised her voice.

"I'm under the speed limit, thank you!" The muscles along his neck twitched. Cathy leaned over to see the speedometer. Damn him, he was right.

"What do you mean it's not good for Amy? Do you mean me? *I'm* not good for Amy?" His blue eyes blazed as he paused at a traffic light. All Cathy could think of was that they had never once exchanged harsh words and now here they were inside his car, where it had all begun, yelling at each other. She felt sick. She had bungled it. She had hoped to be reasonable, to preserve what was good about their relationship. She had hoped they could be friends. She realized now that she had deluded herself.

"We have a beautiful day, with plans for a fabulous night ahead of us, and you announce we're through? What are you, some kind of joker?" His tone was callous, and for a moment Cathy thought of his father.

"No, I'm not a joker," she snapped. "Can't you see how hard this is for me?"

"No, I can't! I can't see a damn thing!" He switched on the car radio to some loud, obnoxious music and drove on, his jaw set.

Okay, so she had hurt him. The execution had been swift and clean. He would heal. Soon he'd forget all about the woman in Ohio with the cute little daughter who wanted to learn to play tennis. Cathy leaned against the door and resisted the temptation to put her fingers in her ears to show her disapproval of his choice of music. Instead, she clenched her fists in her lap and stared stonily ahead as he turned up the dirt lane.

She was dying inside as he stopped the car and waited for her to get out. Had she really expected him to smile, say, "Okay, Cathy, let's have dinner anyway for old times' sake?" Would that have made things easier? But at least he could say something. Was he really going to let her go so easily?

She put her hand on the car doorknob but couldn't bring herself to press it down. Her vision blurred. The barn, the house with the pansies they had planted around the back porch, the swing—everything blurred.

He switched off the radio and they sat in silence. "What happened?" His voice was flat. "Why are you rejecting me this way just when everything was going so well between us? You're just using Amy as an excuse. You know that, don't you?"

Cathy sat for several moments trying to collect herself. "Would you like to come in? I didn't mean to blurt it out that way. We really should talk."

He followed her to the back porch. They avoided the swing. Cathy sat in one of the wicker chairs, and

Robbie perched on the porch railing. He leaned over and ran his hand lightly over the soft faces of the little pansies.

"I don't know," she began hesitantly. "I might feel differently if it weren't for Amy."

"I don't believe that!" His temper flared again as he turned to her.

"Would you let me talk?" She was having difficulty holding on to her own temper.

He relented immediately. "Sorry."

"It's just that she's becoming attached to you. She looks up to you." Cathy floundered. She had almost said "like a father." He bowed his head, and she knew that that detail hadn't escaped him either.

"I don't want her to be hurt when you and I . . . when you leave."

"When am I leaving?" he asked cynically.

"When you graduate."

"Oh." Robbie nodded sarcastically. "Where am I going, since you know everything?"

"Don't be wise," Cathy flared.

"Don't *you* be wise," he countered furiously.

"I imagine you'll move back East to work in your father's head office," she said after a moment.

"You imagine, huh? Why don't you talk about what you imagine instead of just brooding about it? You imagine wrong. I have no intention of moving back East." He met her eyes briefly in a hard, uncompromising gaze, the look of a man who knew what he wanted and precisely how to get it. Although he differed from his father in other respects, in this way they were similar.

Cathy looked away. "Oh." It was all she could say.

"I came to Orange for a reason. I thought you knew that," Robbie reminded her sharply. "I came to familiarize myself with the workers in my father's factories. I came to try to understand why the Midwest has one of the highest unemployment rates in the country and . . . damn it, I came to do something about it!"

His voice had risen in an impassioned cry, but now he continued in a steady, well-modulated voice that commanded both her awe and respect. "I came out here because I'm different from my father. I'm not content to deal with computers. I want to know the people, and I want to increase our productivity through a deeper understanding of the problems of labor. Could you really have forgotten that I told you this?"

"I didn't forget," Cathy said softly, thinking of the conversation she had had with his father. Robbie's passionate dedication was one of the things about him that most stirred her. It was one of the reasons she loved him.

"Then you've decided you don't love me?" His question was an accusation.

She lowered her eyes. She couldn't bring herself to lie about that, but she could choose to remain silent. This was hardly the time to tell him that she'd never thought it was possible to love a man as much as she loved him. But she loved him too much to tie him down.

She had to stop herself from trying to sum up their time together, to put it in a neat little package all tied with a little card that read, *"It's for the best."*

"By the way," she began, hoping to conclude on what she considered an optimistic note, "your father was in town while you were away. He called and we had dinner."

Robbie paled and bolted to his feet. He looked around wildly, as if he wanted to hit something, then let loose a string of violent expletives and sank back down onto the porch, shaking his head slowly back and forth.

"Robbie, it's not what you think," she hastened to tell him, "otherwise I wouldn't have mentioned it. I brought it up only because I wanted you to know that your father loves you very much. He—"

"Then why doesn't he stay out of my life! He had no right calling you. I should never have told him about us. What did he do, try to buy you off?"

Cathy related the story, hoping he would see that toward the end of the evening, his father hadn't been the rigid, unfeeling man he perceived him to be. But his resentment against Raymond Darrow had been built up over a lifetime, and Cathy saw it would take more than a few words to heal the wounds. Still, she felt it was possible. Through her these two men, who were as alike as they were different, might reconcile their problems in the name of a deeper love that bound them.

But there she went again, dreaming of a future— loving wife and daughter-in-law bridges generation gap. She chided herself for having another acute attack of naiveté.

Robbie swatted angrily at a mosquito that was hovering over his bare leg. He frowned and shook his head again, then opened his mouth as if he were about to speak. Finally, though, he kept silent.

Cathy's sigh cut through the stillness, and she leaned

her head back against the wicker chair, trying not to think about the long evening ahead of her. There seemed to be nothing more to say.

"Maybe..." Robbie turned around, his face drawn into a tight, pensive expression. "Maybe," he began again, "we should get married."

Cathy's mouth dropped open, and a thundering in her ears made her think she was about to faint.

- *13* -

DOZENS OF POSSIBLE reasons for his proposal collided inside Cathy, her thoughts spinning in all directions. But one thought stood certain and clear—he had proposed impulsively, out of anger and frustration, and not because he'd considered the idea carefully and was very sure. Tomorrow he would regret his rash suggestion.

His proposal moved her deeply, touching upon her most secret hopes and dreams, but it was all wrong. There were too many strikes against them. She could never tie him down to marriage knowing he would eventually feel constrained and unhappy with her because of all the things he would have given up. She could never marry him knowing she would disappoint him profoundly by refusing to have his children.

When she finally looked up at him, he was standing, his face set in a grim, lifeless expression.

"It isn't a question of marriage." She shook her head feebly.

"Oh no? Then what is it a question of?" His eyes burned into her. "I think you're just afraid," he challenged her. "You're afraid I'll walk out on you . . . like Jed. And you aren't willing to take the chance."

. "That's not true!" Cathy fought back her tears.

"I'm not saying you don't have a perfect right to be afraid." Robbie leaped off the porch and faced her from the lawn.

"Look, I didn't bring this up to choke a proposal out of you." Cathy sprang to her feet.

"Funny, it didn't feel choked out of me." Robbie turned and walked away. "I guess I got carried away," he said with scathing sarcasm. "I could have sworn we were both thinking along the same lines, but I can see I was wrong!" He strode rapidly to his car, his body taut with suppressed anger and frustration, jerked open the door, slid inside, and sped out of the driveway.

She couldn't believe he was gone. She couldn't believe she had actually sent him away. Numb, she went into the house and sat down at the kitchen table. Six o'clock. The empty evening loomed ahead of her— her empty life loomed ahead of her—yet she told herself that she had done the right thing.

She sat without moving, as if any motion might shatter her fragile composure. She sat until finally the kitchen was plunged in darkness, then, scarcely breathing, she wound her way through the dark house and went upstairs to bed.

Her sleep was like death. She awoke on Sunday feeling drugged, her body like lead beneath the covers. She kept her eyes closed. She wanted to shut out everything—light, sound, movement. She drew her knees up against her chest and willed herself to fall back into the dark oblivion of sleep.

When Cathy awoke for the second time on Sunday, she couldn't think, couldn't feel. She moved through the house like an automaton, showering, dressing, making herself some coffee.

Sitting at the round oak table, she told herself she

would have to pull herself together, if not for her own
sake, then certainly for Amy's. The loss of Robbie
would be hard enough on Amy without a disconsolate
mother. So, steeling herself against the numbness
threatening to overtake her, she called Maybeth's house
and, having confirmed it with her mother, told the
girls to get ready to go to the circus.

Later that evening, Susan stopped by the farm. It
helped Cathy to talk, and after a couple of beers, she
felt detached.

"It's for the best," Susan told her.

"I'm thinking of accepting the offer on the farm."
Cathy smiled wanly.

"Don't think of anything now," Susan advised her.
"As soon as finals are over, we're going to the lake.
Why don't you and Amy come along for a few days?"

Cathy agreed, in an effort to stir up some enthusiasm for the future.

The next day she walked through the campus with
her eyes straight ahead, praying not to bump into
Robbie. After giving her last final she stayed up all
night grading papers at the kitchen table.

Two more days went by and the cold, deathlike
feeling still gripped her. Graduation would be on Sunday. She thought maybe she should go to the cere-
mony just to be sure he hadn't gone off on another
tangent, to use his expression. She began to worry
that he was so upset about her that he wouldn't in
fact, be among those graduating. But she knew that
was preposterous. He was too strong to crumble, despite the pain. Like her, he was probably carrying on,
waiting for time to heal the wounds. But the idea that

he was suffering was intolerable. She dialed his number, then hung up before the phone had a chance to ring.

Her resolve was wavering. She strained to catch sight of his car, yearning for any clue that would lead to information about him. She needed to know he was all right.

She began to think that anything would be better than the agony she felt. So what if they got married and he left her in a year or two or even ten? They would at least have had that time. It was foolish to ask for too much. Shouldn't she be satisfied with whatever she could get?

She was ultimately repelled by such thinking. He didn't want a sniveling victim, and she didn't want to be one. Then what was the antidote to so much pain? Only time?

She accepted a date for Saturday night with a friend of Ted's from college. Susan was pleased. She said it showed that Cathy's fighting spirit was returning.

But Cathy returned home late that night drained from making such an effort. She stopped in the kitchen to make herself a glass of hot milk before going to bed and found on the oak table a message scrawled in Amy's red felt-tip pen: *Robbie wants you to call him!!!* The writing was unusually large and the red pen a clear indication of how urgent Amy felt the message was. Cathy started wearily through the dark house. She was glad that Amy was spending the night with Maybeth, otherwise Cathy knew she would have been waiting up to deliver the message in person.

Cathy undressed in the dark and stood in the middle of her bedroom listening to the summer night noises.

Maybe he was calling as a gesture of friendship. It would be nice to end things on a pleasant note. She would always wonder about him, where he was and how he was.

Suddenly she sank to the floor and let the hot tears spill down her cheeks. She had been right about her being afraid of committing herself to another marriage. What if she called him and simply acknowledged that? Not that it would take her fear away, but it might take some of the sting out of the awkward way she had handled their last meeting. She pulled herself to her feet, started for the phone, then stopped. She couldn't risk it. She wouldn't have the strength to turn him away a second time. She fell into a fitful sleep. When she woke the next morning she knew exactly what she was going to do. She was going to sell the farm. It would be late summer before the deal went through, so the sale wouldn't interfere with Marilyn's plans to spend the summer at home.

Cathy returned to the bedroom with a steaming cup of coffee and, propping herself up in bed, made computations on a large yellow legal pad. Maybe, as Ms. Farrell had suggested, she might retain the house and three acres. Although she was considering moving away from Orange, there was no reason to burn all her bridges. Once Amy was grown she might want to return.

She dialed Susan's number, but there was no answer. Of course, Susan and Ted were attending the pre-graduation breakfast.

Anyway it was Sunday. Nobody made real estate deals on Sunday, did they? Cathy drummed her pencil on the yellow pad. Now that she'd decided, she was anxious to start the ball rolling. Jeanne Farrell had given her several New York numbers, and judging by Ms. Farrell's business acumen, she would not be averse to receiving news of such a substantial sale even on Sunday.

Cathy hopped out of bed and located her purse. She was wearing one of Marilyn's oversized T-shirts with an Orange College logo stamped in the middle.

"Anybody home?" She froze at the sound of Robbie's voice. She had been so engrossed in her computations she hadn't even heard a car drive up.

She glanced at herself in the tall oval mirror and saw that her light brown hair was tousled, her green eyes round with astonishment, and her cheeks flushed and pink. Marilyn's T-shirt hit her just above the knees. She gaped at her reflection as if it would tell her what to do.

"Cath? I know you're home. Come out, come out, wherever you are!" Robbie's voice held no trace of resentment. It was as if he had bounded in through the back door with his usual vitality.

"I'm coming," Cathy called as she sorted through a pile of dirty laundry to find a pair of jeans to pull on. She had been too depressed to tackle the mundane domestic chores, and now she looked around her room aghast at the terrible confusion of clothes.

Robbie had caught her totally off guard. She tripped over a pair of tennis shoes and regained her balance. Her heart was thundering though she willed it not to. She tried to drum up some anger along the lines of "How dare you come out without calling first!" but it was no good. The anger wouldn't come.

"Damn!" She began heaving garments around the room in an effort to unearth the elusive jcans. She was bending over with her nose in the wicker clothes hamper when she heard his footsteps outside her room. Seized by a fit of modesty, she tugged at the bottom of the T-shirt and whirled around just as he halted at the threshold of her bedroom.

- 14 -

"HI." ROBBIE LEANED against the doorjamb catching his breath. His eyes were bright, and his face was flushed as if he had run a great distance. He was wearing a smart-looking tan cotton suit and his tie was knotted haphazardly.

Cathy stared at him, speechless. "Hi," she said finally in the same breathlessly cautious voice he had used. She stood with her hands clasped behind her back, her bare legs pressed tightly together, and her feet carefully lined up as if she were a schoolchild trying to pass inspection.

"Amy's not here?" He looked around the cluttered room as if he expected the nine-year-old to crawl out from under a heap of clothes.

His nervousness brought a smile to Cathy's mouth. She caught her breath at the impact his presence was having on her and resisted an impulse to run across the room and throw herself into his arms. She had never been so glad to see anyone in her life.

"Swimming with Maybeth." Cathy's smile broadened.

"Look, Cath, an incredible thing has happened. I...I had to talk to you. Can we? You don't mind?"

He regarded her cautiously, as if he were unwilling to accept her smile at face value.

"I guess we can. Of course."

There was a long pause as they regarded each other. Finally Cathy broke the spell.

"Let's go downstairs." She looked briefly around the room. "A mess, right?"

Robbie smiled and nodded, then his blue eyes saddened as if he realized the unhappiness that had prompted such neglect. "You should see my place," he offered. "What do they say? Sometimes a person has to reach the bottom before he can pull himself together. I think that's what I've been doing, domestically and mentally."

Cathy shrugged, feeling the first inclination toward protectiveness.

"I'll wait downstairs," he said quickly.

"There's coffee on the stove." She stared after his retreating back. The broad shoulders seemed even broader in the tan business suit.

Cathy dug into a bureau drawer and found a pair of cutoffs. Robbie wasn't exactly the type to appear in a cap and gown, smiling into the camera and holding up his diploma for the world to see. A nervous laugh escaped her as she pictured him. She pulled up the zipper on the faded cutoffs, aware that her hand was trembling. Why was she getting so damn excited? There was nothing he could say.

She took a deep breath and stared at her reflection in the mirror. The woman she saw was bubbling over with hopefulness. She picked up her hairbrush and, leaning over from the waist, gave her softly curled hair a vigorous brushing. She reached for a bottle of perfume and checked herself. Only minutes before she had been about to cement a deal to sell the farm, and now here she was primping for an ex-lover.

Ex-lover? No, he wasn't an ex-lover. A week of mourning had not broken the bond between them. On the contrary, seeing him again, she felt that the separation had strengthened the bond. And for him too . . . he had changed. Yes, he had slammed into her house with his usual offhandedness, but she saw that he exerted a new control over his old impulsiveness.

"Stop thinking," she cautioned her image in the mirror. "Go downstairs and hear what he has to say. And be calm."

Her feet still bare, Cathy walked slowly downstairs. She felt oddly as if she were a character in one of her own dreams. She felt herself moving slowly, gracefully, her eyes steady, her expression placid. But she was anything but calm inside.

When she came out the back door he was swinging gently on the porch swing, lost in thought.

"You're not going to graduation?" Cathy asked.

"Not really. Not exactly." He slapped his hands on his thighs, and she saw he was impatient. "But I hope I'm going to be celebrating. My graduation, that is. I'm going to be celebrating but not in the usual . . . the conventional way."

Cathy bit back a smile and shook her head. "I have no idea what you mean." She padded over to the swing and sat down.

"I'm getting to the point." He turned to her as he reached for something in his pocket. "I'm not sure about the order of things here, but please bear with me."

"Robbie . . ." Cathy protested as he handed her a small box. She could see it was a jewelry box, and was once again put off balance by him. She began to shake her head and made no move to open the little box.

"Like I said, I'm not certain about the order of things..."

"Robbie..." Cathy rolled her eyes. She had always known he was a determined young man, but this was ridiculous.

"Damn it, listen to me!" He took her hand and held it. "I had breakfast with my father today."

"So?" She fought against the longing she felt with his hand gripping hers.

"He was very impressed by you." Robbie looked at her intensely.

"What does that mean, he was impressed with me? He wants to hire me? Your father doesn't have anything to do with us." Cathy tried to stifle a rush of optimism.

"Of course he doesn't have a damn thing to do with us. But *you* had something to do with my father and me, and that's one of the things I wanted to tell you."

"What do you mean?"

Robbie looked away, seeming to weigh his words carefully. "I've uh...been involved in a little power struggle with my dad that you didn't know about. It uh...related to you." He shook his head irritably. "I'm sorry." He looked at her earnestly. "I bungled things the other day, Cathy, and the reason I'm so hesitant now is that I've got about three things to say to you and I want to say them all at once."

"That's not possible," she told him, finding his earnestness both touching and irresistible.

"I know." He nodded. "So I'll say what's most important and you have to promise not to interrupt."

"I can't promise," Cathy said honestly. "If we're going to have a conversation, then we both have to feel free to say what comes to mind. But I promise not to run into the house and slam any doors in your face."

Robbie grinned and a ripple of pleasure ran through her as he squeezed her hand.

"First, I love you." He looked at her steadily. "There's no one else I love, no one else I can imagine loving as much as I love you." A lump began to rise in Cathy's throat. Robbie began to run his forefinger along the back of her hand. "I love you because you're thirty-four "

"Five," Cathy corrected him gravely.

"Thirty-five. Because you've struggled and made a good life for yourself and your family. If you were twenty-three you wouldn't be the woman I love. You couldn't be at twenty-three. I love Amy too, because she's a reflection of all the strength I see in you."

He paused and Cathy started to reach out to him. She stopped herself and turned away. "All these things are nice to hear," she said gently, "but . . ."

He put his forefinger on her lips to silence her. "I had this little box in the glove compartment of my car when we had that terrible fight last week. I guess the reason I got so mad was because I'd planned . . . I'd planned to ask you to marry me that night."

Cathy lowered her eyes. It had honestly never occurred to her that he might have intended to propose to her all along, hadn't asked her to marry him impulsively, on the spur of the moment. He must have been devastated when, just as he was about to ask her to marry him, she announced they were finished.

"I'm sorry," she said with tears in her eyes.

"And I was too damn proud to produce the evidence."

"But, Robbie, I really meant what I said." Cathy looked away for a moment to compose herself. "Look, I've seen the way you are with children. I stood in the side yard at Susan's house and watched you romping with her kids. And Amy adores you."

"Cathy, I don't care!" He took her hands urgently. "Maybe I needed a week without you to know for sure, but I don't care about anything except us sharing our lives together. It's you I want. It's you I need, not any children we might have."

"You just think that way now..."

"No," Robbie protested quietly. "No, this is not an impulsive conclusion. I *know*. If you don't feel the need or the desire for children, then I don't either. And I understand how you feel. You've spent your life being responsible for others, worrying about four children, bringing up two on your own. You should have what *you* want now. I just hope you want me."

"I do want you!" Cathy cried in a choked voice.

"And that's the most important thing." Robbie's eyes pleaded with her. "Do you know how lucky we are? Do you know how many people would die to feel the ease, the closeness that we felt from the beginning? You can't ignore that. It's too rare, too precious, and you know it."

Cathy nodded slowly. Of course she knew it. The emptiness she had felt over the past week had been almost unbearable. "I missed you so much." There was a note of awe in her voice.

"I don't need to have children with you to be happy,"

he said softly. "I need you, here in this house that you love. And it's crazy how much I love Amy. And you know what else? I've been having daydreams about Marilyn and Bruce and Brian, about meeting them and getting to know them. So you don't have a reason for not marrying me, Cathy," Robbie concluded with a circumspect smile that held a trace of a suspicion that he was going to emerge victorious.

"I don't?" Cathy asked tremulously. "I don't have a reason for not...?"

Robbie drew her against him and held her. She could feel his body throbbing with excitement. "Marry me, Cathy, and let us live a life according to our own needs and the needs of the family you already have."

"You're sure?" she whispered, still unable to comprehend what was happening.

"Yes." Robbie lowered his mouth to hers, and she yielded to the profound gentleness of a kiss that seemed to probe into her very soul.

He drew back and looked deep into her eyes. "This week was torture for me."

"It was for me too." She drank in his blond, aristocratic good looks with a new sense of wonder.

"How soon?" he asked as he massaged the small of her back.

"How soon what?" She felt dizzy as he slid his hand under the T-shirt and ran his fingers along her spine.

"The wedding. How soon? Tomorrow?" He spread his fingers beneath the shirt and practically covered her entire back with one hand.

"Tomorrow!" Cathy's eyes flew open.

"By the little stream that runs through your woods."

He brushed his lips against her neck, and she felt heat prickle all along her scalp. "We'll send dad's private plane to pick up Marilyn. The rest of the children can take a day off from school."

"You've planned it all?" Cathy cried incredulously.

Robbie smiled. "You can wear that sexy off-the-shoulder dress you wore to Susan's party."

"Have I said yes?" Cathy tilted her chin upward in a seductive gesture.

Robbie ran his hand under it and down the smooth line of her throat. "I think you have," he said huskily.

"Yes!" Cathy raised herself up and put her arms tenderly around his neck. "Oh, yes!" She pressed her parted lips fervently against his. "Where's that little box you've been carting around? I want to open it." She was laughing and crying at the same time. She kissed him again, feeling a delicious warm arousal flooding over her as he slipped his tongue slowly inside her mouth and ran it searchingly along the roof. Cathy's own tongue shot forward to titillate and tease until the impact of what was happening made her pull back and look at him with dreamy eyes. He was the most beautiful man, a man who would keep her forever guessing in the best sense, yet she trusted him implicitly.

"Maybe not tomorrow." She smiled as she twisted around on his lap to locate the little box. "Marilyn has finals this week. She'll be home next Sunday."

"We can make plans," he responded eagerly. "Dad will just have to fly back."

"Your dad! That's right, you said you had breakfast with him." Cathy was distracted from opening the box.

Robbie nodded, once again serious. "We had the best conversation we've ever had. Maybe the only conversation. Usually one of us leaves rather abruptly."

"I'm glad." Cathy smiled warmly.

"What did you say to him the night you two had dinner?"

She shrugged. "I have no idea. I just said what I thought. Why?"

"Well, he still doesn't agree with me, but he's giving me a fighting chance. First, he's reinstating the men he fired, and second, he's agreed to use them as a control group to test my theories."

"That's fabulous!" Cathy threw her arms around his neck. "But I didn't do anything."

"You must have said something." Robbie touched her chin fondly. "He even asked about you, casually of course. Didn't want to go overboard in approval."

Cathy laughed. "I think there's hope for both of you. Actually I think your father's on the shy side. He gives the appearance of being cold and stern, but I think he's just . . . uneasy."

"Well," Robbie jostled her impulsively, "don't expect me to agree with his archaic ideas."

"I think you'll convince him." Cathy grinned as she directed her attention back to the little velvet jewelry box.

"You look so fetching in that outfit." Robbie ran his hand around her bare knee. "Maybe you should be married in cutoffs. We could wade into the stream in our bare feet and—"

"Robbie, it's the most beautiful . . ." Cathy threw herself into his arms.

Robbie removed the ring from the velvet container

and slipped it onto her finger. "Emeralds to match your eyes." He looked pleased. "And one single diamond which is forever. How's that for planning? And some speech too, if I do say so myself."

Cathy admired the wide gold band, which was inset with a string of small emeralds and one large diamond.

"I bought it in New York," he said. "This has been in the works for a long time. And there's something else."

"What?" Cathy felt near to bursting with happiness.

"Remember I said I couldn't figure out the running order of today's agenda?"

She nodded, relishing the suspense.

"How close were you to selling the farm, Cathy?" He eyed her smugly.

"What?" She looked bewildered.

"Big business," he declared. "Big business headed by Raymond Darrow. My dad was the one who made those first offers."

"You're kidding!" Cathy's mouth flew open.

"Nope. It's true. He wanted to build a plant here."

"Here?" Cathy looked around at her beloved house and barns. "It's not zoned commercial."

"That never bothers my father. Business morals are not his strong suit, but as I said, reformation may be possible. He would have purchased the land under some other auspices and later made a deal with the town zoning committee. It's been done before."

"Did you know this when we first met?"

Robbie shook his head. "No. I just knew he was looking to buy up more land around here. I felt there were more appropriate tracts of land available in other towns. I even made several suggestions, but he rejected them. Too expensive. Cheaper to make a high offer to some unsuspecting private citizen. He's not a crook. It's legal, it's just not fair. The fact is, he didn't even know whose land he was trying to buy until that Saturday he and I had the blowup. It was all being handled through his lawyers. It's not the way I like to do business, and through my private channels I happened to learn what was going on. That's why I flew to New York and that's why I sent Jeanne Farrell out to make another offer. All Susan knew was that Jeanne was representing Darrow Enterprises, and that there were now two bidders on the farm."

"But why?" Cathy was puzzled.

"To pull a fast one on my dad? Yes. But mostly so you wouldn't lose this place. I kept waiting for you to mention it to me so I could simply talk you out of it. But you never did, secretive person that you are." Robbie toppled her against him and hugged her. "It must have been much on your mind, Cath. I wanted you to trust me enough to really talk to me about it, but since you didn't . . ." He looked at her emphatically. "I decided to top dad's offer, sew the deal up for myself, and give it back to you."

"Incredible!" Cathy's astonishment was reflected in her entire body as she moved back to look at him. "You really have been busy."

"I know." Robbie grinned. "I wouldn't have let you lose this place, even if things didn't work out between us. Hell of a guy, aren't I?"

Cathy's eyes brimmed with tears as she placed her hand affectionately on his shoulder. "You are. You really are, Robbie."

"One of a kind, wouldn't you say?" He teased her

with the same cocky smile he had worn the day he had found her and her old Dart on Route 71.

"I can't believe it." Cathy gazed at him with a dazed expression. "We're really going to be married?"

Robbie gathered her up in his arms. "Yes, we really are." He slipped his hands under the roomy T-shirt and rested them lightly on her breasts. "Let's go inside." He gave a low moan as her nipples hardened beneath his fingers.

"What about graduation?" Cathy teased.

"Best graduation I've ever had." Robbie stood up, pulled her to her feet, and bent down to kiss her.

Cathy surrendered to the delicious sensation of his warm lips. How easy it suddenly seemed, how inevitable. She had no doubts, no fears. This, she knew, was a love that would grow and endure.

They entered through the back door, sliding their arms around each other's waists, and walked through the cool dining room toward the stairs. A slow smile played on Cathy's lips as she glanced up at Robbie's profile. How incredible! Suddenly the idea of having a child, his child, seemed like a real possibility. She ran her hand around the outside of his muscular thigh as they walked down the upstairs corridor.

"What are you thinking?" He gave her a curious smile.

"You'll see." She smiled up at him.

"I hope so." He hugged her firmly against his lanky body as they entered her bedroom . . . their bedroom.

Second Chance at Love

All of the above titles are $175 per copy

Available at your local bookstore or return this form to:

SECOND CHANCE AT LOVE
Book Mailing Service, P.O. Box 690, Rockville Cntr., NY 11570

Please send me the titles checked above. I enclose _____ .
Include 75¢ for postage and handling if one book is ordered; 50¢ per book for
two to five. If six or more are ordered, postage is free. California, Illinois, New
York and Tennessee residents please add sales tax.

NAME _____

ADDRESS _____

CITY_____ STATE/ZIP_____

Allow six weeks for delivery.   **SK-41**

WHAT READERS SAY ABOUT
SECOND CHANCE AT LOVE BOOKS

"Your books are the greatest!"
—*M. N., Carteret, New Jersey**

"I have been reading romance novels for quite some time, but the SECOND CHANCE AT LOVE books are the most enjoyable."
—*P. R., Vicksburg, Mississippi**

"I enjoy SECOND CHANCE [AT LOVE] more than any books that I have read and I do read a lot."
—*J. R., Gretna, Louisiana**

"I really think your books are exceptional... I read Harlequin and Silhouette and although I still like them, I'll buy your books over theirs. SECOND CHANCE [AT LOVE] is more interesting and holds your attention and imagination with a better story line..."
—*J. W., Flagstaff, Arizona**

"I've read many romances, but yours take the 'cake'!"
—*D. H., Bloomsburg, Pennsylvania**

"Have waited ten years for *good* romance books. Now I have them."
—*M. P., Jacksonville, Florida**

*Names and addresses available upon request